SHOOTING STARS

Border marshal Rafe Monrow is in the deadly El Diabolo desert, fleeing the ruthless Ford Cable and his cohorts ... Three days earlier, Monrow had ridden into the seemingly peaceful town of Panhandle — but Panhandle is home to a dangerous band of smugglers and before Monrow knows what is happening, every gun is aimed at him. Now the man with the tin star pinned to his chest fears for his survival. It seems his hunters like nothing more than shooting stars ...

DALE MIKE ROGERS

SHOOTING STARS

Complete and Unabridged

LINFORD
Leicester

First published in Great Britain in 2012 by
Robert Hale Limited
London

First Linford Edition
published 2013
by arrangement with
Robert Hale Limited
London

A catalogue record for this book is available
from the British Library.

ISBN 978–1–4448–1742–3

Published by
F. A. Thorpe (Publishing)
Anstey, Leicestershire

Set by Words & Graphics Ltd.
Anstey, Leicestershire
Printed and bound in Great Britain by
T. J. International Ltd., Padstow, Cornwall

This book is printed on acid-free paper

Dedicated to my lovely friend Maxine Hansen

Prologue

The arid border between Mexico and its northern neighbour stretched from one ocean to another. Over 1,000 miles of mostly uncharted terrain had become nearly forgotten by the powers that be since the end of the brutal Civil War. There had been more important things on the minds of those who ruled in their ivory palaces back East. Wounds to be healed. Wounds which would never truly heal. For the memory of those who had fought in either grey or blue would be long. Very long.

It was some time before it occurred to anyone in Washington that where there were borders there was also likely to be contraband and therefore lost revenue. The long, meandering unmanned border had offered outlaws and bandits alike numerous opportunities to smuggle and make their fortunes.

1

And they had taken them.

Apart from men rustling and smuggling things back and forth in and out of both countries there was also the problem of rampaging Apaches, who did not recognize either of the governments that had laid claim to their ancestral homelands.

It had taken seven years for the conquering north even to consider engaging anyone to man the border. When it did only a small team of men was hired to become border marshals. The word 'small' was indeed justified: in fact there were only four of them to police a distance of more than 1,000 miles from the Pacific to the Gulf of Mexico.

Their job was to try and stem the flow of goods in either direction by whatever means they could. It was a futile exercise and yet when governments think they are losing vital tax dollars to hardened bands of criminals, common sense evaporates as swiftly as teardrops on a desert floor.

Rafe Monrow was one of the quartet

of men assigned to bringing the rule of law to those who had lived their lives without it.

He had drawn the short straw and was assigned the most dangerous and deadly 500-mile stretch. With his star gleaming in the Texas sun the border marshal had spent most of his time simply riding along the unmarked border, vainly searching for those he was meant to bring to heel.

Not once in all the time since Monrow had been appointed a marshal had he come close to seeing or finding anyone who remotely aroused his suspicions. For the border was long. Too long for just four men to control successfully.

But Monrow had always tried to please his distant paymasters.

Then one fine morning, identical to a hundred which had preceded it, the border marshal neared a small, tranquil-looking town set just a mile north of the Mexican border. The town was unthreateningly called Panhandle. It seemed to be sober and respectable, but that would prove to be a mirage.

Months of uneventful riding had lulled the young horseman's senses into a state of total indifference. He had realized months earlier that it was virtually impossible for a solitary rider ever to be in the right place at the right time for catching any lawbreakers.

As Rafe Monrow would violently discover, neither the town nor the majority of its residents were as friendly or peaceful as they first appeared to be.

Panhandle was a place where men with stars pinned to their vests were not welcome. Without even realizing it the border marshal had found what he had been searching for.

Like a lamb to the slaughter Monrow had innocently steered his black gelding straight into what he would soon discover was not a law-abiding settlement at all, but actually the most dangerous place a man wearing a tin star could ever ride into.

They had a hankering in Panhandle to shoot at stars; or at least, at men wearing them.

4

1

The bleached white sands of El Diablo never ceased moving. Like phantom sidewinders they twisted and turned across the surface of the flat desert plain in all directions. To those whose brains had been baked beneath the incessant sun they appeared to be driven by unseen forces: forces which lured those naive visitors towards a place that only the bleached bones of death ever managed to reach. This was no place for anything with warm blood in its veins. No place to ride into willingly unless you had a hankering to die a long lingering death. Yet for some there was no choice but vainly to seek sanctuary in the inhospitable shimmering heat haze beneath that merciless sun. It was either that or face the men who had chased you into this satanic place. Men with their guns hot from blasting lead venom at the fleeing rider.

This was a land of nothing but death. No Eastern map-maker had ever dared venture into it. On their maps there was nothing but a blank section with the printed words EL DIABLO DESERT..

El Diablo was well named.

Only the Devil himself would have felt at home in this unholy part of the West. The bowels of Hell itself could not have been hotter. Even the intrepid Apaches had left it to the creatures who somehow managed to exist beneath the unrelenting sun. They were wise enough to want no part of the parched barren land.

For as far as the eye could see there was nothing but flat, dry sand. Baked for a hundred centuries, it seemed to have become something else: something as hard as granite, with a fine layer of animated sand granules upon its surface. Even the sky across the desert appeared to be dead. Blue, but dead all the same. No clouds ever filled this sky. Even scavenging vultures were smart enough to avoid El Diablo.

Smarter than the lone horseman.

What lay out there in the uncharted depths of this lethal desert? the rider silently wondered. Out beyond the wall of shimmering haze. An oasis? Or just an end to his long hard flight from the guns of those who refused to stop hunting him as though he were little more than vermin.

His eyes narrowed and surveyed what lay ahead of him and his weary mount. Whatever lay out there was masked by the cloak of the stifling haze. He managed to raise himself up until he was balancing in his stirrups over the wet mane of his horse. If there were mesas or mountain ranges ahead of him he sure could not see any sign of them. He lowered his aching body back down upon the soaked leather of his saddle.

Rafe Monrow knew it was no good turning back and retracing the trail which had led him to this lethal landscape because the riders were still on his trail. Just like the shifting sand which kept moving ceaselessly around the legs of his now exhausted black mount, those who were tracking him would never quit. Not until they had killed him.

He lowered his eyes and looked at his star. It was flashing as the brilliant rays of the sun danced across its surface. All of his troubles had been caused by that small tin star, he thought to himself. There were some places where the law was greeted with open arms, but he had managed to find a place where the opposite was true. The star had been little better than the bullseye on a target. It had drawn lead like flies to a jakes.

Monrow eased himself up off the sweat-soaked saddle and threw his right leg over the cantle. Slowly he allowed his weight to bring his aching body back down to the ground. He felt as though someone had broken every bone in his tired body. He steadied himself.

The last time he had stood on the

ground it had been upon sweet grass that swayed around his spurs. He had managed to fill his canteens in a spring as he watched his pursuers gaining on him. Now there was nothing under his boot leather but the strange sand which moved as though actually alive.

He was tuckered. More damn tuckered than any man has a right to be without falling down dead. He glanced back at the wall of moving air. Although he could not see them he knew they were still there. Still coming with their long rifles.

Folks were meant to respect the law, he sighed. Not try to shoot it.

His pants were soaked and the salt he had lost from the long three-day chase burned the cracked flesh beneath his saddle-weary pants. He stared at the canteens which hung from the horn of the saddle and was about to lift one from its perch when he recalled that it was empty. They were both empty. They had been empty for the last twenty-four or more hours, after he had filled his hat bowl and allowed the black horse to finish their meagre rations.

Monrow dragged the bandanna from his neck and rubbed the salty sweat crust off his face. Again he looked back. The hoofmarks left by his horse were all there was to see. Nothing else had come this way for the longest while, he thought.

Not even a wild critter had been loco enough to venture here.

Maybe that was good but he knew the opposite was more likely to be true. Nothing had ridden this way for a damn good reason. That reason was all around him. Who but a madman would ride into the bowels of Hell?

His were the only tracks because other critters had more sense than to head into a place more akin to a furnace than anything else he could imagine. Even sidewinders probably gave this land a wide berth. If there was life out here he sure could not see it.

Monrow rested his back against the horse and looked up. There were no clouds anywhere to be seen. Just a pale-blue sky that looked as though even it was fading as the giant sun kept on burning. He rubbed his throat. It was dry. Dryer than it had ever been before this moment. He felt as if all of the moisture in his tall lean frame had been sucked out by that relentless sun. He was hurting like a man just kicked by a mule.

How long could anything with blood in its veins live without water? The question began to haunt him. How long would it be before he too became bleached bones?

The man turned and with faltering steps moved to the head of the faithful horse. He held on to the bridle and tried to look the animal in the eyes, but he could not. The poor pitiful creature was spent, just like its master. It, like him, had given its all in the long flight away from the dozen or more riders who continued to pursue them. The lathered sweat was falling from the tall horse like snow.

Guilt began to gnaw at Monrow. It was fine for a man to run headlong into a place where only death was certain but not right for a faithful animal to be forced to suffer the same fate.

Monrow knew that it would be kinder to put a well-aimed bullet between the eyes of the horse. Kinder than allowing it to keep on suffering. The man turned away from the trusting eyes and glanced all around, as though searching for something to give him a fragment of hope.

About a hundred yards away from horse and master the haze rose and encircled them. It was like a shimmering screen. A wall of mocking mystery. Everything beyond it was masked. Monrow tried to swallow but there was no spittle. He lowered his head and placed a gloved hand on the grip of his .45. For the first time in his life Monrow felt that everything was over. He had run clean out of hope.

He slid the gun out of its holster and eased the hammer back until it locked into position. If there was another choice he sure could not see it. If there was salvation to be found it was masked by that wall of shimmering boiling air.

Monrow inhaled deeply. The fiery air burned his lungs. The horse was finished just like him, he kept silently telling himself. It had brought him as far as it could and now deserved to die with dignity.

Rafe Monrow continued to look away from the trusting horse as he raised the gun until its barrel rested against his shoulder. He could still smell the aroma of the showdown he had been forced to participate in back at Panhandle. The scent of gunsmoke remained in the barrel of the .45.

He glanced at the horse. It had never faltered, unlike so many other nags he had seen over the years. For five years the handsome creature had done everything the rider had commanded it to do. Never once had Monrow been bucked or had call even to think about the creature beneath his ornate saddle.

Now it was dying of thirst like him.

More sweat suds fell from the

emaciated horse. Monrow rested the gun barrel against the temple of the tall horse as he drew the bridle down.

The rider's eyes returned to those of the horse. Both horse and master stared into one another's souls. This was the hardest thing Monrow had ever had to do. If the poor creature had bust a leg or something, Monrow would not have hesitated. He would have dispatched the animal swiftly so that its suffering would end quickly.

Yet this was different.

Damn different.

Could he kill the horse just because he sensed a lingering death awaited them both? Maybe the bullet would be better placed between his own eyes, Monrow pondered.

Suddenly he heard the sound of the men who were hunting him as though he were nothing more than a fox and they were a pack of hounds with the scent of their prey in their nostrils. Monrow moved away from the head of his horse and lowered the .45 until its barrel slid back into its holster. The sound of the horsemen carried on the hot air and swept over him. They were getting closer, he thought. Closer with their long rifles and venomous hearts. He squinted back across the trail his horse had left. The heat haze prevented him from seeing his followers but he knew they were still coming.

Still relentlessly coming.

'Why won't ya quit?' Monrow yelled out into the dry air. Suddenly a volley of bullets passed through the curtain of hot air and flew over his head.

Without even thinking Monrow grabbed the horn of his saddle and threw his weak body back on top of the high saddle. He gathered in the reins as more shots whizzed around them. He drove his spurs back into the flesh of the horse and the black responded as it had always done.

The half-dead rider and his equally spent horse thundered on into the swirling wall of hot air.

Neither of them was ready to die just yet.

2

A million demons could have secreted themselves unseen within the choking dry mists which had engulfed the arid desert around the fleeing horseman and his charge. Yet there was only one reality which both of them recognized, and that had nothing to do with mythical imaginings. It was the lethal tapers of gun lead as they tore through the air in search of their target. On and on Monrow forced his horse to try and escape the venomous fury of the deadly bullets. Deeper and deeper they went into the unknown mist where perhaps sanctuary might be found. Even total exhaustion could be defeated when you were scared enough, the rider thought. There was no spur sharper than total fear.

It was as though every drop of moisture hidden far beneath the sand was being drawn out of the ground by the incessant sun far above them. The strange swirling vapour engulfed the horse as its beleaguered master ignored his own pain and forced the pitiful animal beneath him on towards their unknown destiny.

The firing continued. Monrow knew the bullets were being fired blindly by those who wanted to ensure he never again visited their remote settlement. For whatever reason they kept shooting their long-barrelled rifles behind him. The deafening sound became entangled in the hot air and encircled the rider. As the black horse forged on blindly into the suffocating desert Monrow wondered what these seemingly honest men feared so much that they wished to put paid to him. What was going on back at Panhandle that required such drastic and bloody action?

After what felt like an eternity the noise of their rifles began to diminish in intensity as Monrow drove his spurs back into the already scarred flanks of the resolute animal. The hot tapers of lethal lead ball no longer kept pace with the loyal horse. He looked back and kept on urging the spent creature on into the blinding mist. Monrow knew he ought to stop and allow the black horse to rest, but fear had now gripped his innards.

The shooting might have stopped for the moment but he knew that they might catch up with him again at any time. He continued to whip his reins across the shoulders of the horse as his spurs drove back into its flesh.

'C'mon. Keep going,' he implored.

For a while that was exactly what the exhausted gelding did. Mile after mile the pitiful creature managed to thunder through the almost foglike heat haze deeper into El Diablo.

Then the loyal animal staggered in mid-stride of its long legs. Monrow felt it shake beneath his saddle. As though shot by an invisible arrow it fell forward. Within a split second the rider found himself flying helplessly over the neck of the animal as it ploughed heavily into the soft, hot sand. As the black horse crashed headlong into the ground Monrow felt his boots leave their stirrups. He somersaulted through the boiling air before slamming into the sand. Monrow had hit the ground hard and rolled over a half-dozen times before coming to a painful halt.

Dazed, Monrow lay where he had fallen for over five minutes. His outstretched left arm pointed back to where he had been ejected from the saddle. As he managed to regain the wind which had been punched from his lungs, he slowly curled around until his knees were beneath him. The reins were still wrapped around the fingers of his gloved hand.

For what felt like a lifetime, Monrow sucked in the hot air and rested. If anything was broken he sure could not feel it. He dropped both hands on to the sand and started to crawl like a toddler back to his mount. There were no marks on the sand between himself and his horse. As he kept on moving like a whipped hound towards the animal he began to realize how far he had been thrown. More than fifteen feet, yet he did not seem to have broken a single bone.

The man with the star pinned to his shirt stopped when he found the head of the horse. He rolled on to his rear and rested his head on his raised knees. This was a good place to sit, he thought. Sit and stare at the crumpled horse who had vainly tried to match the speed its master had wanted it to find.

There was a peculiar quiet around the area. The hairs on the nape of Monrow's neck started to rise as his eyes searched for an explanation to why he felt so uneasy.

His fear of what lay behind him with primed Winchesters now took second place to what might actually be here hiding in the soup like boiling fog.

Where the hell was he?

How far had they gone before the horse had failed?

His mind silently screamed inside his still dazed skull. Were there things out here in this deadly desert that were as lethal as his pursuers' bullets? Maybe there were Indians, he reasoned. He had not set eyes on an Indian since before the war. But that did not mean they no longer existed.

Maybe there were strange animals in El Diablo, of a design he had never imagined, not even in his worst nightmares. Something was out there.

He could sense it.

Maybe it was just the fact that he was starved of the precious liquid he craved. Folks went loco when they were dying of thirst. Maybe his mind was playing tricks on him. He was being slowly killed by this damn desert, he cursed angrily. Sweat was rolling off his head as though he were standing beneath a waterfall.

The heat had not relented. It still bore down and surrounded him. Monrow released his grip on the long leathers and shook his head. He patted his soaked hair and wondered where he had lost his hat.

'Damn it all,' he swore, knowing that without a hat his brain would be broiled in half the time. He glanced up; the sun was still high and still lethal.

The body of the horse was twitching as all dead things tend to do until they finally realize that they are dead. It was a sickening sight.

Somehow Monrow managed to get back to his feet. He staggered a few paces, then fell over the long legs of the prostrate creature he had literally ridden into the ground.

He lay on his face and chewed on the dry sand. Was there any point in attempting to stand up again? he asked himself. After all, he had no place to go.

Monrow scrambled back to his knees and wiped the sand from his cracked mouth.

'Maybe I ought to just stay here and wait,' he muttered to himself. 'Wait here for them *hombres* to come and finish me off.'

Suddenly out in the haze he heard a sound.

Faster than he would have thought possible he drew and cocked his .45 and aimed its long barrel to where he thought the noise had come from. Then another brief but chilling sound filled his ears.

He had been correct.

He was not alone.

3

There were eighteen of them. A mixture of various types normally found shackled in chains further north. Yet here they remained free because the law had never managed to subdue or overwhelm them or their enterprises. Men from both sides of the long border were driven on by the same unseen force. Money. There was a lot of it to be made by those who took what they wanted from anyone unable to protect their rightful belongings. Trade in precious gems and ore had never been so profitable in the aftermath of the long brutal war to the north and a series of revolutions to the south. Money could be made when you managed to cut the law out of the equation.

A lot of money.

The riders looked respectable enough beneath their variety of headgear. Any onlooker might have even considered them to be a posse on the trail of a ruthless outlaw, but appearances were often as deceiving as the men themselves. This was not the first occasion that Ford Cable had led his fellow Panhandle citizens after an innocent victim into the uncharted depths of El Diablo in order to protect their hides and livelihoods. It was however the furthest any of them had ever been forced to venture into the desert.

Rafe Monrow was proving to be a hard man to kill compared to those who had gone before him.

The sands whispered around the hoofs of their mounts as they pressed on after the trail left by the black gelding. Each horseman knew that the same sand had already hidden each of their previous transgressions.

Armed with the newest repeating rifles and twice their number of well-notched six-shooters Cable and his followers rode on. It was imperative that the border marshal be stopped before he had a chance to relay the information he had gained from Panhandle to the authorities. The last thing these hardened riders needed was a troop of cavalry invading their territory and imposing martial law upon them.

The black-hearted horsemen rode on into the suffocating mist that mocked them. Each was determined as the others in his resolve to catch and kill their prey.

There was no other way.

Not in their collective book anyway. Rafe Monrow the border marshal was doomed to die. Each of the horsemen was more than willing to execute him himself.

For most men who skimmed across the border in either direction there was no law but gun law. No law that might bring them to book. The elusive horseman who had fled under a volley of deadly lead had suddenly brought the truth to their black hearts. Rafe Monrow had made them realize that he was the law. The man with a star who could and would bring them into line and curb their lawless lives.

But it had been a naive and foolhardy assumption that people want to be honest citizens. Some men desire nothing more than the thrill of outwitting those who draw up laws in distant places and throwing them back in their faces.

Panhandle had risen from the barren soil with no help from those who proclaim themselves to be rulers of all that they have marked out on their maps. The people within the boundaries of the small, prosperous settlement had created Panhandle themselves with the cunning that had created the nation. They did not intend to allow a distant government to steal it away from them. It had taken blood, sweat and a whole wagonload of tears to make it what it was and none of its people wanted it to change.

Rafe Monrow had discovered that the hard way.

The arrogance of youth had been

given a bloody nose and no mistake. It had all gone terribly wrong for the border marshal. He had found out that the gleaming star on his chest might mean something to those who gave a hoot but not to these folks. To them it was exactly what it was.

Merely a tin star. Nothing more and nothing less.

He had never imagined that the seemingly peaceful-looking settlement he had ridden into so openly was quite as corrupt as it ultimately turned out to be. For the faces of those who lived within its limits appeared no less law-abiding than any others he had set his eyes upon over the previous three years during which he had worn the star. In fact they had seemed to be even friendlier than the usual bunch he encountered. The people of Panhandle had actually seemed to welcome his arrival.

How wrong Monrow had been.

He had allowed complacency to overrule his once natural instincts.

Monrow had been a fly who did not even notice the deadly web he had ridden into.

Rafe Monrow had made himself a victim. He had been unable to realize that many men and women get used to a certain way of living their lives, even if it is a lawless way. They become set in their habits and will fight to the death to remain as they have always been.

Whatever it might say in the vast volumes of law, they will fight. When liberties are removed, even when they are questionable liberties, folks get dangerous.

It had all started three days earlier.

Three days which now seemed to the exhausted Monrow like a lifetime ago. As the blazing sun continued to beat down upon the marshal and fry his brain, a delirium swept over him like a tidal wave. His once rational thoughts started to become frayed and confused. Then and now blurred into one. Reality slipped through his fingers like the dry sand which surrounded him.

He stared into the relentless heat haze.

Panhandle had given no outward appearance of being anything but a normal town, like thousands of others set along the long unmarked border which separated Mexico and the states and territories which lay to its north.

In fact it had everything a peaceful settlement should have, even a sheriff's office and an appointed lawman and deputy. Business after business filled the store fronts as Monrow had progressed down the main street astride his tall mount. Each appeared to be doing good trade with the thousands of people who made their way up and down the long thoroughfare.

Monrow had never even imagined what he was riding into. There was no hint of what lay in the cold hearts of the seemingly honest people he studied from his high perch.

Never judge a book by its cover, the old saying goes. How true that proved to be. If only he had not fallen into that trap things might have been so different. So very different.

For years he had done the same thing in so many towns along the border. Not once had he met any trouble or defiance. Maybe all those other towns had been secretly praying for salvation from those who preyed upon them.

Panhandle had been different.

He had been sent by a distant government to inspect the numerous settlements, to check whether they were managing to survive after the long bloody war which had torn the country apart for so many long years.

A border marshal was rare, but he had the same authority and power as a federal marshal. The small star pinned to his brushed leather vest was meant to protect him.

Yet Monrow had discovered to his cost that a tiny tin star had no power to protect its bearer if those who set eyes upon it do not respect what it and the man wearing it stood for.

Three days earlier Monrow had

considered himself a knight in shining armour, sent to champion right against wrong.

Now he knelt beside his dead horse wondering if he would see that devilish sun set again. His confused mind tormented him almost as much as the relentless rays which beat down on his sweat-soaked form.

Then he heard the strange noise again.

What was out there?

Perhaps nothing at all. His hands clutched at his head and tried to shake the confusion from his mind. His eyes narrowed but all they could see was the strange fog which surrounded him.

Then his heart began to pound.

What if the Devil was coming to get him?

Monrow managed to get back on to his feet as he listened to the haunting sound which whispered all about him and the dead horse.

Was El Diablo about to add his bones to the others scattered all around the desert? Had the Devil decided it was time to swat this intruder?

It was getting hotter. The bowels of Hell itself could not be this hot, Monrow silently thought.

The haze seemed to be getting closer.

The whispering encircled him.

'I'm in big trouble,' Monrow managed to croak. 'Killers on my tail and who knows what that is up ahead?'

4

Seventy hours earlier it had been Ford Cable himself who had first noticed the spiral of trail dust rise up into the blue sky as the lone horseman rode steadily towards Panhandle. In an otherwise cloudless sky it had been like a beacon alerting the town's dark-hearted souls that a stranger was about to enter their midst. Cable had not shown any concern to all those who surrounded him outside the freshly painted façade of the Rolling Dice gaming-house. He had seen many drifters come and go in his time. Why should he expect this rider to be any different from those who had preceded him? As he considered the rider his mind drifted back to the few unwanted men who had made the mistake of coming to Panhandle. Lawmen. They had been sweet-talked and then, when they discovered too much, dealt with.

Cable dragged a match down the wall, cupped its flickering flame and sucked in the smoke from his cigar. He tossed the spent match out beyond the hitching rail and nodded as a half-dozen of his contemporaries talked. The poker game had lasted all night, and as usual Cable had won more than he had lost.

The sun was still rising over the small town as he continued to nod without actually listening to anything his cohorts were saying. For as the rider headed down the long avenue towards the eastern outskirts of the town something else had caught Cable's keen attention.

At first the burly man had not realized what it was that drew his full attention. Then he saw the glinting of the tin star pinned to the rider's vest. Like a mirror it reflected the dazzling rays of the sun and flashed to those who were alert enough to see it.

Cable saw it.

Without allowing any of those who

surrounded him to see his concern Cable walked to the very edge of the board-walk and leaned a shoulder into the brightly painted porch upright. Studying the approaching rider with eagle eyes he rested his full weight on the wooden pole and savoured the smoke he held in his mouth until he was certain that his assumption was correct. This was a lawman who was riding into his town.

'We got us company, boys,' Cable drawled slowly. He pointed the smoking cigar at the horseman who was getting closer with every heartbeat.

The others had consumed a lot more whiskey than Cable had and were not as alert as the man who had made himself their unelected leader long ago. Each of them looked to the outskirts of their neatly ordered town and the long winding trail which led down to it.

'It's just a drifter,' a voice said through a yawn.

'A drifter who just happens to be wearing a star, boys,' Cable pointed out.

This time his words found their mark. Each of the men looked with more interest to where Cable was indicating. Each of them felt his jaw drop as their sore eyes focused into the morning sunshine.

'Am I right?' Cable asked.

'Damn it all,' one of them cursed.

'What would the law be doing in Panhandle, Ford?' Strother Duke asked his far larger friend. 'I thought we'd seen the last of them troublesome varmints.'

'How can ya be sure it's a lawman, Ford?' Brody Barr queried from behind his thick eyeglasses.

Cable tapped ash from his cigar, then returned the expensive smoke to his mouth. He gripped it firmly with his teeth. 'Hell. He's wearing himself a star. Can't ya see it glinting out there?'

'Might be spectacles in his vest pocket.' Barr shrugged.

'It's a star.' Cable sighed.

None of the others could see as well as Cable but they knew that if he said the rider was wearing a star then it was certain that he was.

A tall slender man with hair as white as snow named Bo Fontaine nodded as he rested a weary hip on the hitching rail. 'Ya reckon he's lost, Ford?'

A chuckle rippled through the tired card-players.

Only Cable remained unmoved by the humour. 'There's only one way to handle a star-packer.'

Again the men chuckled.

'Ain't nothing I likes more than shooting stars.' Duke grinned as he rested a hand on his holstered gun grip.

'Yep,' Cable agreed. 'Ain't nothing like shooting a star-packer.'

Fontaine pulled his Colt from its holster. 'Can I kill him, Ford?'

Cable thought about the question for a while, then slowly shook his head. 'Reckon not. I figure we ought to try and hoodwink the critter first. Try and get him to leave of his own accord.'

Fontaine thrust his weapon back into its holster. 'Damn it all. I got me a hankering to kill me a star-packer.'

Ford Cable turned and looked at the men who flanked him. He pointed at Duke. 'Go get Sol and tell him to put his sheriff's star on, Strother. Maybe this lawman will be easier to fool than the others.'

'Where is Sol?' Duke asked.

'Try the Lady Jane,' Barr suggested, aiming a finger across the street at the lavishly decorated brothel.

Strother Duke gave out a wistful laugh. 'That boy will die in that place.'

'That's a fair bet considering he spends most of his time there,' Barr agreed.

As Duke stepped down into the street and started across its wide distance Cable returned his eyes to the rider. 'Got me a feeling in my craw that this star-packer will be as ornery as all the others, boys.'

The men all nodded.

The shade of the branch canopies felt good to the horseman who had spent the previous week or more riding along the sun-bleached border. Rafe Monrow had allowed his black gelding to find its own pace on the approach to Panhandle. The tall black gelding had caught the scent of fresh water and started to move faster.

'Looks like a nice peaceful place,' Monrow had said to his mount. 'Yep. A real nice quiet place.'

5

The bell that tolled in the whitewashed church tower at the very end of the long street ought to have alerted Monrow, but he was tired. Dog tired. The ears of the black gelding had risen though and turned towards the place which in itself was yet another creative façade. For there was no holy man within the white building preaching the virtues of good over evil. No preacher proclaiming his message as he shook a well-thumbed Bible to a cowering congregation. It was just a building with a massive hand-carved cross mounted on its tower.

The bell continued to toll as Monrow kept his horse walking deeper and deeper into Panhandle. It was a warning to all those who had yet to set eyes upon the intruder wearing a star. If he had been the sort to carry a pocket watch he might have realized that, but the dust-caked marshal had never seen a need for him to know what the time was. Nature had always provided him with enough information. When the sun rose it was time to get up and when it set it was time to sleep.

Monrow did not even know what day of the week it was. Out on the sun-baked trail one day blended into another for those who travelled the relentless length of the border. All the young rider knew for sure was that for the first time for weeks he might be able to drink something other than water. His flared nostrils had already smelled coffee brewing as the aromatic scent of his favourite beverage drifted from open windows and doors. A cold beer might also go down well and wash the sand from his mouth, he had thought.

Wrongly his weary mind considered that he had again found something close to civilization. A place where you could rest and savour the better things denied to men who rode the long lonely trail between Mexico and his homeland.

Every eye was glued to the horseman who steered his faithful mount along the main thoroughfare. Monrow imagined there was only curiosity in their curious souls. How mistaken he was, for what he took to be simple curiosity was actually hatred. Each of them would have killed him there and then given half a chance. Men, women and even the children knew that trouble was riding the lathered-up black gelding. The star pinned to Monrow's chest gleamed in the rising sunlight like the target it actually was.

Each of them looked to where Ford Cable was standing beside his favoured henchmen. They knew that whatever was to happen, it would be started by the well-built man who sucked on his cigar and silently watched the unwanted visitor to Panhandle.

If Rafe Monrow had not been so weary after the lengthy ride from the last border town he might have been aware that the eyes which watched him were burning into him like the rays of the sun. There were no friendly smiles of welcome, for these people had only one collective emotion and that was to see him dead.

This was a missionary who was destined for the pot.

Caked in scores of miles of trail dust the horseman looked the worse for wear. He was tired and it showed in the way he allowed his charge to make its own pace down the middle of the busy street.

As though drawn by a magnet the horse turned and aimed itself toward the long trough below the boardwalk where Cable and his cronies were standing. For some unknown reason it had dismissed the half-dozen other water troughs it had passed before it had chosen the one outside the Rolling Dice from which to quench its thirst.

After stopping the gelding lowered its long neck and then began to drink from the trough as its master leaned back and studied those who had already inspected every part of the border marshal.

'Howdy,' Monrow said before pushing the brim of his Stetson back to reveal the tanned line across his temple a mere inch below his hairline.

Only Cable ventured a reply. 'Howdy.'

Monrow sighed and carefully eased himself off the saddle before lowering his tired frame down to the street. As his horse drank he looped its reins around the hitching pole and secured it.

'I'm the border marshal,' Monrow uttered before looking at the men's faces in turn. 'Name's Monrow.'

Again Cable was the only man to respond. 'Howdy, Mr Monrow.'

'Long hot ride from San Remo,' the lawman commented as he watched his horse continue to drink.

'Reckon it must be.' Cable nodded through a cloud of grey smoke. 'Ain't never bin there myself. Heard it can be a tad hot this time of year.'

Monrow removed his bandanna and wiped the dust from his features. He looked far younger than any of the men who studied him had imagined.

'I'm here on official duty.' Monrow dipped the bandanna into the sparkling water and rubbed his sore neck.

'Figured as much.' Cable said.

'You got a mayor in this town?'

Each of the men shook his head.

'Nope,' Cable answered. 'We ain't never seen the call to have us no overpaid lard bellies stealing our hard-earned money. Got us a few saloons and whorehouses though.'

A grin crossed Monrow's newly revealed face. 'Heard them varmints called a lotta things but that's the best one yet. I reckon most of them are lard bellies.'

Cable forced a false smile. 'You said official business. What does that mean exactly, Mr Monrow? What kinda business does a star-packer have in a place like Panhandle?'

The border marshal gave out a long sigh. 'The government sent me to see if there might be illegal trade going on across the border.'

Fontaine glanced at the younger man. 'Why?'

'Why? It ain't legal, that's why,' Monrow replied.

Fontaine looked away and slowly nodded. 'Oh.'

'Smuggling's a mighty bad thing,' Monrow added. 'Folks gotta pay their taxes so the government has money in the treasury.'

'And what does this government do with the taxes, sonny?' Barr asked. 'I'll tell ya. It wastes it all on war.'

Monrow raised an eyebrow. 'I just enforce the law. Ain't nothing to do with me what them lard bellies back East do with the revenue.'

'Seems kinda corrupt.' Cable sighed.

'Is there any smuggling going on in these parts?' Monrow pressed.

Ford Cable allowed the ash to fall from his cigar, then brushed it away with the back of his left hand. 'Nothing like that happens in Panhandle. You might as well head on back to the trail yonder and find another town.'

'I will when I'm satisfied,' the marshal said firmly.

Cable grinned. It was not a grin which denoted humour in the black soul of the well-built man, but something else. Something far less easy to evaluate. 'Good.'

'You got a hotel in this town?' Monrow enquired. His gloved hands toyed with the reins he had just tied to the long, twisted pole.

Brody Barr stepped between Fontaine and Cable and pointed along the street. 'Down beyond that clump of trees. Right next to the livery. Can't miss it.'

Bo Fontaine tilted his head and stared hard at the young lawman. 'If ya happen to get a room there, I'd keep ya window shut if'n I was you.'

The border marshal gave a slow nod and tugged the reins free before leading his horse away from the trough and starting for the hotel. 'Thank ya kindly, gents.'

Ford Cable chewed on his cigar. 'Happy to oblige, Mr Monrow.'

There was something in the way

Cable had said his name which made Monrow pause for the briefest of moments and he glanced back at the sturdy character. It was as though he were being threatened or warned. Monrow did not say anything before continuing along the street to where he had been informed he would find the hotel.

The men kept their eyes on him until he turned the corner and disappeared from sight.

'Ya should have let me kill him, Ford,' Fontaine drawled before spitting. 'He's just like all the others. He's trouble and no mistake.'

Cable rubbed his chin.

'Maybe so.'

6

The interior of the Black Heart saloon was filled with the most powerful and dangerous men in Panhandle. None of them was more powerful than the burly Ford Cable, who remained silent as he poured himself a full three fingers of rye into a large glass tumbler. Unlike all the others Cable had suddenly noticed the date on the tobacco-stained wall calendar. He alone had recalled that at any time a shipment of silver would be rolling into Panhandle from across the nearby border. Mexican silver of the highest quality which he and his partners would sell for ten times the price they had paid for it.

Cable rubbed his chin, downed the whiskey in one throw before igniting a match with a thumbnail and bringing its flame to the end of his cigar. He puffed, then refilled his glass as his mind raced. Monrow might be only a youngster compared to himself, but the boy had the full authority of the law behind him. He was here for only one reason and that was to put an end to all the illegal activities which had made Cable and his cronies rich beyond most men's dreams.

The smoke lingered around the head of the brooding man as he listened to all the others in the bar as they spewed out their own ideas as to what to do with the star-packer.

There was no way of knowing for sure when that shipment of silver would arrive. It might happen today, tomorrow or even next week. Driving heavily laden prairie schooners from the depths of Mexico to Panhandle had never been a precise science at the best of times.

Why had Monrow ridden into town now?

Of all the times he might have arrived here he had chosen now to make things even more tense. Cable had no qualms about killing a man wearing a tin star, but if he were able to outwit the critter it would be better. Lawmen were like rats. Kill one and suddenly another turns up.

If he could get that marshal to ride out satisfied that nothing illegal was happening in Panhandle he would then go searching some place else. Give grief in some other border town.

Cable looked at the others in the bar. Fuelled by whiskey the talk was big and getting louder. It was as if every single one of the men who had become wealthy by moving goods back and forth across the border knew that the stranger in their midst might be far more dangerous than he looked.

They talked of just killing Monrow but Cable knew men like the young marshal took a lot of killing.

Cable had listened to all of the frantic talk for nearly an hour since the marshal had left them outside the Rolling Dice. He had not uttered more than an occasional sigh. When men of their breed became nervous things tended to get a little tense. Cable had lost count of how many of them had waved their guns in the air as they bragged of how they would kill Monrow given half a chance.

When would the shipment of silver arrive? Cable remained standing at the very end of the long bar counter, with his left boot on the brass rail. He kept watching the swing doors beyond the crowd. It was only when Strother Duke burst back into the saloon that the town's leader moved away from the bar and strode toward his sweating underling.

'Well? What did you find out, Strother?' Cable asked the breathless man who accepted his leader's drink and downed it in one swallow.

Duke ran a sleeve across his brow. His eyes darted to all of the faces which were watching and listening.

'I seen him stable his horse and tell the liveryman to rub the critter down after feeding it,' Duke stated. 'Then he told old Joe to make sure the nag was saddled at around eight.'

The audience moved closer.

Cable ran his fingers down his face as he considered the information. 'What in tarnation does he want the horse readied for after sundown?'

Duke edged closer. 'That ain't all.'

'It ain't?' Cable raised an eyebrow. 'What else did you learn?'

'He took a room which overlooks main street and had a bath.' Duke said, pointing back over his shoulder. 'After the bath he went to the window of his room and stood looking down on everyone passing below. The critter seemed to want to keep an eye on the whole lot of us.'

Cable shrugged. 'Reckon there ain't nothing unusual about that. He is a snoop, after all.'

'He don't seem normal to me, Ford,' Duke ventured.

'Why not?'

'He ain't even given none of the whorehouses a second look and no mistake.' Duke nodded firmly. 'What

54

sort of real man rides all that way and don't even have himself an itch? Ain't normal, Ford. Ain't normal at all.'

'We ought to just kill him,' Bo Fontaine said wearily. 'The man deserves killing. He's trouble.'

'I got me a feeling that this critter is even more serious about catching us out than the last couple of star-packing varmints were, boys.' Cable returned to the bar and lifted his bottle. He took a long swig, then shook his head slowly. 'They at least took themselves a bit of time to service a couple of the girls. This boy just seems too serious.'

'And what about the wagons of silver, Ford?' Barr piped up. 'Have ya forgotten that we got us a real valuable cargo coming at any time? What if they turns up when he's marching up and down the street?'

'I ain't forgotten about the silver.' Cable snorted.

Fontaine placed a cigarette between his lips and ran a match up the side of his pants. He cupped its flame and sucked in the smoke. As it drifted back from his mouth he leaned over to Cable.

'Ford, I figure this boy might be a whole lot more trouble than any of the other bastards who've poked their long noses into our business,' the silver-haired man commented. 'Ya should have let me kill him earlier, Ford. We might not get another chance that sweet.'

'If he needs killing we'll get our chance and we'll take it,' Cable vowed. 'I already got a few boys perched on the rooftops with Winchesters, Bo. They'll unleash their lead if'n I give them the signal.'

'But what about the silver?' Barr repeated.

'Seems to me we have to send a rider or two out to try and intercept the wagons before they arrive,'

Cable replied. He stared into the smoke of his cigar as it twisted and turned around his fingers. 'Trouble is we don't know which route they're taking.'

Strother Duke gave a powerful nod. 'Can I go and try and find them, Ford. Can I?'

Cable rammed the cigar between his teeth, clenched his fists and rested them on the damp bar counter as his eyes stared at the mirror behind a stack of glasses. 'Yep. Take a few boys with ya, Strother. Take provisions. Don't come back until you find them wagons. When you do locate them tell them to make camp. We don't want them turning up until that marshal is out of the way.'

Duke was eager. He grabbed a couple of men close to the saloon's door by the arm and took them with him.

A general rumble of laughter went around the saloon.

Only Cable did not laugh.

'We gotta be smart,' Cable warned. 'We already killed us a couple of lawmen and covered our tracks so nobody even suspected Panhandle. But if we ain't careful we might just find a whole army being sent here and that would end our days of doing business over the border for ever. They might build a fort. Nope. Killing Monrow has to be our last option. We have to give him a lotta rope, boys.'

'Folks hang themselves when they got enough rope,' Brody Barr added with a smile.

Cable nodded again. 'Right.'

'Trying to look innocent is gonna be mighty hard for us to do.' Fontaine spat at a spittoon. He missed.

Just at that moment Sheriff Sol Cannon entered the Black Heart and paused as his eyes adjusted to the dim interior of the saloon compared to the sunbathed street. He rubbed the sheriff's star on his shirt and made his way to the bar. 'Whiskey.'

The crowd surrounded the man who still had the stale perfume of the whorehouse lingering on his clothing.

Cannon glanced over the heads of those between himself and Cable. He nodded.

Ford Cable pushed his way through

the others until he reached the man who actually looked like a man of the law, though the total opposite was closer to the truth. 'Ya gonna do what I told ya, Sol?'

'Yep.' Cannon nodded.

'Good.' A wry smile covered the features of the town's most dangerous soul as he patted the shoulder of the taller man. 'I reckon we got all our backsides covered.'

'Damn right,' Cannon agreed.

'You boys finish this rye.' Cable handed his whiskey bottle to the others and straightened his hat, then headed towards the doors. 'I'm gonna check around town and make sure there ain't nothing in the stores to make Monrow figure he's hit paydirt.'

'Ya mean all that silver and gold we done bin paid with for rustling all them steers and selling to them Mexicans?' Brody asked.

'Yep. That and all the other valuable cargo we've smuggled over the years.' Cable winked as both his hands hit the swing doors apart and he marched out into main street. 'Panhandle gotta look tame and as pure as a virgin's bloomers.'

Fontaine watched the doors of the saloon rock on their hinges as the burly figure went out into the afternoon sunlight. He filled his own glass with the fiery whiskey, studied it for a while, then downed it. 'I still figure it'd be a lot easier to just kill that marshal right now.'

Every one of the heads nodded in agreement.

7

The blazing sun was starting to set somewhere out beyond the array of neat structures which made up the settlement known as Panhandle. There was only a short time before it would disappear, leaving a black velvet sky filled with sparkling jewels. Monrow had watched with interest the three men who had rushed into the stables earlier and then thundered out towards the desert. Apart from that brief moment of urgency the town had remained quiet. He had not given Strother Duke and his cohorts a second thought.

There was something else for him to brood upon. Something which twisted his craw as if warning the youngster that this town was not as it seemed; that it was a place where star-packers came to die.

Monrow had decked himself in fresh clothes from his saddle-bags after a hot bath. His long fingers had carefully buttoned up the front of his shirt whilst his eyes continued to watch from the room window. Little escaped his attention. He knew that many people hated anything to do with the law and it was obvious that Panhandle was no different. He stood by the open window of his hotel room and studied the town and its people from his high vantage point.

There was a glowing red in the sky as though the heavens were aflame. Its devilish illumination seemed to paint everything below it in the same scarlet hues.

People were moving back and forth as they went about their rituals, yet Monrow had noticed that each and every one of them glanced upward at his room window and straight at him. There seemed to be contempt in every unsmiling face. It was as though an unwelcome guest had arrived in their midst and they awaited his departure eagerly.

The border marshal had witnessed many things in his short life but Monrow had never felt quite so uneasy before. He carefully pinned the star to his fresh shirt.

The gentle breeze which moved the lace drapes to either side of him made Monrow recall his home. A home he knew was gone for ever. The war had destroyed many things and one of them was his past. He reached to the dresser and dragged the heavy gunbelt off its surface. He strapped it on and tied the leather laces around his lean right thigh. He checked the .45 in its well-oiled holster. It still slid up and down easily. Ready to be drawn and fired.

For the first time since he had purchased the weapon he wondered whether two guns might be better than just the one. Until now he had not actually required even the one, but Panhandle seemed to pose an unseen threat that one six-shooter might not be able to cope with. Monrow rubbed his neck with the palm of his hand. For some reason he felt as though every one of the people in town hated him, or perhaps hated what he stood for.

Panhandle was an enigma. It gave every outward appearance of being an ordinary law-abiding settlement like countless others throughout the West, but was it?

He knew many places did not like strangers but that was not what made him fretful. There was a genuine threat here and he was only just starting to realize it. What these people did not want within the boundaries of their town was anyone wearing a tin star.

Monrow sighed. Was it just the imaginings of a tired mind? He inhaled deep and long and caught the aroma of cooking as it drifted on the late-afternoon air. He pulled the drapes away and spotted the café with its smoking chimney a hundred yards away.

'Ya just hungry, Rafe boy,' Monrow

had told himself as he turned away and faced the door. Then he recalled the strange feeling which had swept over him when the large Ford Cable had simply uttered his name. Again Monrow checked his .45, then slid it back into its resting place.

His stomach began to growl.

He was hungry. Hungry for real vittles.

Dry biscuits and jerky had been his diet since leaving the last town. Now his mouth filled with saliva at the prospect of sinking his teeth into steak and eggs. Monrow had always been a man of simple tastes and requirements. He had never longed for a fortune like some men do. All he wanted was to be allowed to live his life the way he chose.

Apart from the two sets of trail clothes, his gun and his black gelding, he owned nothing. His entire fortune filled one pocket of his pants: a few paper bills and some coins. It had always been enough.

The war had taught him the true

worth of possessions and money.

He had seen a lot of structures rased to the ground. He had also witnessed many Southern banks blown apart by Yankee cannons. The sight of money floating in the acrid air above the mindless carnage and destruction was something he would never forget.

What good was money when you had been sent packing to meet your Maker? Enough money to buy vittles was all any man could truly need. That and a good gun and an even better horse.

Monrow tightened the knot of a clean bandanna under his chin and placed his freshly brushed Stetson back on his head. The tall young man who had entered Panhandle without realizing he was about to face danger equal to anything he had endured during the brutal war was ready to venture back out into the busy town.

He locked the room door behind him and then made his way down the long staircase to the lobby of the quiet hotel. A half-dozen men sat around the spacious room, hidden behind news-papers.

Only three days earlier Monrow had walked out into the street without a clue to the fact that at least half a dozen rifles were trained on his every movement from various roof tops.

He kept on walking until he reached the closest of the many small cafés Panhandle boasted. Just as he gripped the handle of the door his attention was drawn across the street to a large wooden structure which seemed out of place.

The marshal stepped down from the boardwalk and made his way across to the building. He stopped just short of its tall double doors and looked upward. It was big like a livery stable but it was no livery stable.

A warehouse?

Across its large doors a massive chain with three padlocks seemed out of place. There were no windows. Above the doors the name of Ford Cable was painted in large letters. Monrow moved closer to the doors. There was a gap of maybe an inch where the doors did not quite meet. The young man leaned towards the gap and vainly tried to look inside. He then stared down at the ground and noticed it was well beaten up with wheel-rim tracks in and out.

He was confused.

Suddenly a voice from behind him made Monrow swing around. It was Cable chewing on another large cigar.

'Can I do anything for you, Mr Monrow?'

Monrow could feel his hand instinctively hovering above his holstered Colt.

'I was just wondering who Ford Cable is,' he replied.

'You happen to be looking at him.'

'What is this building?' Monrow aimed a thumb at the large structure.

'It's mine,' Cable replied through a cloud of smoke. 'That's all you need to know.'

'But what is it? What is it used for?'

Cable brushed ash from his vest. 'You know what they say happened to the curious cat, don't you?'

'Is that a threat, Mr Cable?' Monrow stepped closer to the larger man. His eyes narrowed but there was no fear in Cable. He defied anyone to make him back down. 'I don't like being threatened.'

'Just remember what happened to the cat.' Cable blew smoke at Monrow, then turned and walked away along the boardwalk in the direction of a saloon. The big man glanced up at the rifle barrels poking out from rooftops. He smiled.

The border marshal had wanted to continue questioning the arrogant man but then he felt his stomach start to grumble again under his shirt. He bit his lip and started back across the street towards the café and the meal he knew awaited his silver dollar.

'I'll get my answers one way or the other, Mr Cable,' Monrow whispered to himself.

Then, as he gripped the door handle of the café he suddenly noticed the reflection in its glass panel. He paused but did not turn. The reflection of the two riflemen on top of the building behind his wide shoulders was unmistakable. For the first time Monrow realized that if he made one false move it might be his last.

Swallowing hard, Monrow entered the café.

8

The deafening sound of rifle fire resounded through El Diablo as the lethal tapers cut through the mist. Monrow was reined back from the depths of delirium and the memories of what had occurred only three days before. He instinctively ducked as he felt the heat of the bullets pass all around him. The whirlpool of memories was dispatched and evaporated as he tried to make his once fertile brain work.

More shots came through the mist behind him. It sounded like a swarm of hornets passing all around the place where he knelt.

Monrow coughed. He could taste blood in his throat. He rolled on to his hip and panted like a hound as he tried to keep his thoughts on the present. He rubbed his throat.

He needed water damn bad.

Every swallow ended in the taste of bloody spittle. Monrow looked all around him as though he was beginning to doubt the reality of where he actually was. To his baked brain he was still back in Panhandle headed for a café and that juicy steak resting beneath a couple of over-easy eggs.

Was this real?

He had heard tales of Apaches torturing white men. Surely they could never have come up with anything as bad as this, he thought. This was horrific by anyone's yardstick.

Again he managed to focus on the dead horse beside him.

Damn it all. That had been the best nag he had ever saddled and ridden. Defying the shots of his pursuers Monrow forced himself back up on to his knees and rested both hands on the saddle.

Steam was rising from the body of the lifeless horse.

Even the dead were not spared from

the merciless sun. It kept on dragging the very last drop of moisture from its helpless victims.

Monrow knew he ought to remove the saddle and take it with him, but it was pointless. He was too weak and it was far too heavy. He ripped the canteens free and somehow managed to hang them over his shoulder.

The stifling mist had surrounded him. Now he could see no further than just beyond the horse's body. When had it encroached to within a mere few feet of where he knelt?

Monrow went to remove his Winchester, then recalled that he had lost that precious rifle back in the town days before he found himself here. The fingers of his gloved hands still inspected the scabbard under the saddle, though. Just in case that was a dream.

What was happening?

He scrambled back to his feet and hovered like a drunken man ready to drop back to the ground. He hurt. The bruises from the fall he had suffered when his horse had burst its heart had matured. Monrow looked at his arms. They were blackened by the bruises.

He must have been unconscious, he thought.

Bruises never show that fast.

For how long had he been knocked out?

A chilling realization swept over him. It must have been hours. Hours of which he could not recall one second.

The men who were following his tracks had kept on chasing their prey and made up a lot of distance in that time. More shots flew out of the mist. Monrow wanted to return fire but knew that would only let Cable and his cronies know where he was.

Monrow had to escape, but was escape even possible?

He wearily pressed his bruised left arm against the empty canteens. If he did happen to find water in this unholy desert he could at least fill them up to prolong his agony.

For that was all his fevered mind

could think about. Not escape or salvation, but death. Inevitable death. It was waiting for him and even water would only delay its claiming him for a short while.

Then in a brief lull in the firing he heard a strange haunting sound out in the fog. He swung on his heels and almost fell as he gripped the gun again and tried to aim its barrel to where the noise was coming from, but it was no good.

The sound was everywhere ahead of him. Masked from prying eyes by the pervasive mist. What was it that mocked him? Why could he not just die quickly as his faithful horse had done?

Monrow staggered forward towards the sound. His index finger stroked the trigger of his drawn Colt.

It was creeping like an invisible evil sprite ahead of the place where he was standing. The gun began to shake in his hand when he caught another sound in his strained ears.

It was riders.

Their horses' hoofs were pounding in the hardened ground beneath the fine veneer of moving sand.

It was the men who were hunting him.

They had closed the distance on him just as he had thought they must have whilst he was asleep. Soon they would open up with their rifles again and this time he knew that they would not miss.

Terror gripped his heart again and squeezed real hard. Whatever it was making the eerie noises ahead of him was no match for the real bullets of those riders. Even Monrow's befuddled mind knew that Ford Cable would not be satisfied until they had killed him.

The border marshal thrust the gun back into his holster. He forced his legs to obey and walk away from the noises of the approaching hoofs. He moved into the malignant mist like a jack rabbit trying to avoid a pack of hunting hounds.

Somehow Monrow began to run.

9

The café had provided a meal fit for any passing royalty and yet the border marshal had not truly enjoyed one mouthful of it. He had forced it down and mopped up the steak-and-egg juices with a chunk of well-torn bread until his plate gleamed, but something deep inside him was twisting and cutting into his thoughts. He knew that there were rifles ready to cut him down at any given moment and that moment could probably come sooner rather than later. Defiantly, or perhaps just stupidly Monrow had chosen the table next to the window that gave on to the main street; he knew that the rooftop marksmen would have no trouble picking him off with the lantern lights behind him. Yet he was not truly afraid. He had witnessed a lot of death in his time. Far too much for someone of his tender years. Monrow knew it could be swift or slow, but it would come some time to all who graced the earth. It was the only true certainty.

Why had they not fired? He had given them ample opportunity to do so and yet they held their Winchesters as though waiting to be ordered to act.

That was it. They were awaiting the command to fire. Like mindless creatures they could not act unless someone told them to do so. Like sheep they were helpless unless their leader gave them the nod.

Cable.

Monrow knew it had to be Cable. He was the leader who issued decrees of life and death in Panhandle. Without him they were just a bunch of headless sidewinders. This town had a lot of secrets and the keeper of those secrets was the cigar-chewing Ford Cable.

The young marshal knew he was right but that made his job no easier. No less dangerous.

He lifted his coffee cup to his lips

and sipped at the black beverage. It tasted a lot better than the trail coffee he had been drinking for the previous couple of weeks. As he set the cup down in its saucer he glanced around the one-room café with its ten identical tables. Each table was surrounded by four hardback chairs. Another room beyond sight was where the food was cooked by the handsome female who had not spoken a single word since he had entered her establishment.

All she had done was stand in the doorjamb between the two rooms and watch him like a hawk. Monrow had attempted to draw her into conversation, to try to learn something of the town he had found himself in, but it had been a futile exercise. She only made noises and watched.

He was alone and knew that no other customer would enter whilst he sat by the window. A score of men and women had passed that window and each of them had looked as though they would have entered if it had not been for

Monrow's presence inside the popular establishment.

Perhaps they knew something he did not. They might know that bullets might start flying into the glass panes at any time.

It was now almost dark outside. Monrow tilted his head back and screwed up his eyes as he looked across the street at the tops of the roofs opposite. He could just make out movement against the sky of stars. The men were still there, he thought. Still there ready to fire their rifles.

The young man rose and dabbed the napkin against his mouth as his thumb and forefinger searched for a silver dollar. He placed it down on the table-cloth. He looked to the female and smiled but there was no response.

She remained stony-faced.

He pulled his gloves over his wide hands and lifted his Stetson off the chair next to one he had warmed for the entirety of his stay in the café. He placed it on his head and tightened its drawstring. He touched its brim in salute.

'Fine meal, ma'am. Mighty fine.'

There was not a trace of gratitude for his remark in her face. The expression remained exactly the same. It was as cold as all of the others he had seen in Panhandle.

He turned the doorhandle, pulled it towards him and stepped out on to the boardwalk. A cold shiver traced over him and he knew it had nothing to do with the temperature. Panhandle was warm with the heat of the desert which flanked it.

The street was aglow in the amber light of a dozen streetlamps on high poles and three times that many store-front lights that cascaded their illumination on to the sandy street. Rafe Monrow pulled the door until it closed behind him and then out of the corner of his eye, caught sight of the female rushing from the back room towards it. She dragged its blind down and turned the key in its lock. The window blind was lowered a moment later. He stood in the relative darkness of the store front and surveyed the area again. Were there other men with guns aimed at him somewhere along the thoroughfare, he had wondered.

Monrow rested the palm of his right hand on the grip of his .45 and inhaled deeply. There was only one way to find out and that was to walk along the boardwalks to see. After he had gone about 200 yards Monrow spied a flickering lantern hanging next to a shingle that protruded from a wooden wall. His keen eyesight could read the single word painted upon it.

'Sheriff'.

So there *was* law in Panhandle, he recalled thinking. But what kind of law? The regular kind or the kind that made a mockery of everything the law stood for? He knew he would find out.

The sound of Winchesters being cranked echoed around him, and he started to sweat. This job was not as easy as he had once thought it was. Not if it were done properly, anyway. The town was bathed in more light than he had seen for many a long year. They sure had more than their fair share of coal-tar oil, he concluded.

He was about to start walking when again his attention was drawn to the large building directly across the wide street. Only Ford Cable's warehouse was dark and devoid of anything resembling life.

Then he saw the rifle-toting men high above it and knew that there had to be something of value within its high wooden walls.

But what?

Cable looked like a man who had himself a fortune.

But how did any honest man make a fortune in these parts? The question troubled Monrow, for there was only one answer. An honest man could not.

Of all the towns dotted along the endless border he had accidentally stumbled upon the one which was breaking the law, probably on a scale he could never calculate.

Monrow knew his suspicions had to be right. On the ride into Panhandle the border marshal had not seen a single head of cattle. The land beyond this oasis did not look fit to graze anything on. So how could anyone get rich?

There was only one way.

Every man and woman in Panhandle was involved in smuggling Mexican goods across the border and selling them for vast profits further north. That was why they had not welcomed him with open arms, for each and every one of the varmints was tainted with the same brush.

His mind recalled how he had been told that thousands of head of steers had been rustled from ranches a hundred miles north of this innocent-looking town. Folks could make a lot of money rustling Texas longhorns and selling them south of the long, remote border.

Monrow knew he had found the very

place his superiors had wanted him to find.

Yet there was no satisfaction in the belly of the marshal. Only the realization that he might have bitten off more than he could chew by arriving alone. If he was correct and the entire town was involved in the profitable enterprise, he was in far bigger trouble than he had ever imagined possible.

How does one man stand against a whole town?

Monrow let out a sigh and aimed his boots in the direction of the Black Heart saloon. As he walked along the boardwalk he suddenly realized that he could not hear another living thing in the whole length of the street.

His eyes darted all around him.

Main Street was empty but Monrow could feel a thousand eyes burning into his very soul from the windows and doors. His pace was steady but he knew that meant nothing. He felt as if he were walking towards a gallows.

Only the sound of his spurs kept him

company. Out of the corner of his left eye he could see the marksmen keeping pace with him from their lofty perches.

A bead of sweat rolled down from his hatband and negotiated his jawline before dripping on to his bandanna.

He had never desired a fortune, but now he started to wonder whether forty dollars a month was enough for a man to face a whole town full of potential executioners.

His hand pushed the swing doors apart.

Monrow entered the Black Heart.

10

It sounded like the battlefields of Hell itself to the parched mind of the desperate border marshal. White-hot tapers came from out of the mist behind him and hissed like a bag of vipers as they passed his weary form. The heat of each lead ball was a reminder of how close he was to meeting his Maker. Once more he had been dragged from his memories back into the reality of the insane situation he had somehow found himself sucked into.

Monrow was running for his life. Even dazed and starved of water his brain kept on telling him to keep running. To pause for even the blink of an eye would be to die.

Cable and his small army were still hunting their elusive prey. Still riding after the man with the marshal's star.

Still eager to kill him.

The sound was growing louder as hammers fell on the brass casings of their rifle bullets. No man could outrun horses for ever, he told himself. If the mist lifted and they could see their prey he was finished.

Bullets kept tearing through the fog from behind the fleeing marshal as his stiff legs somehow continued to run. Monrow could feel his heart pounding inside his chest like a war drum. The shots had been above him at first, then following volleys had seemed to be level with his thrusting elbows. The young marshal tried to concentrate. How were they managing to keep their lead coming at him without being able to see him?

It was his boot tracks.

Ford Cable's men were shooting in the direction his tracks led off into the fog. That was it, he told himself. He had to change direction fast. Without a second's hesitation Monrow turned and started to run to his left. Their bullets would continue to follow his original path until they reached the place where he had altered direction. By then, he told himself, he would have changed direction again.

Monrow could still not see a thing.

He recalled the frost from the night before. It had been an inch thick and covered the entire desert. Now it was evaporating as the sun sucked up every ounce of El Diablo's moisture. He kept forging on.

The fog was his only protection.

His only shield.

Fine granules of sand filled his mouth and eyes but he did not slow his pace. A satisfaction filled his head as he listened to their bullets being fired in the wrong direction.

Their confusion did not last long.

Less than two minutes later the ground around his high heeled-boots exploded as rifle lead cut up the terrain to either side of him. A chill overwhelmed Monrow. They were even closer than he had dreaded. They had already reached the place where he had turned.

He kept on running. The lack of water seemed to be seizing him up with each painful stride of his long thin legs.

'Keep going!' he snarled to himself as he zigzagged like a sidewinder across the sand.

Exhausted, Monrow tripped and fell but somehow managed to stumble back on to his toes without even missing a step. They would have to work a tad harder if they wanted him dead. Again bullets were passing him like crazed hornets. He changed direction again. He knew that the bullets were now travelling far beyond him. The marshal realized that that meant the horsemen were closer than they had ever been to his dust-weary carcass.

'Keep going,' he spat. More rifle shots rang out through the haze. 'They're shooting blind.'

He altered course again. He had no idea where he was or towards what he was headed. Then the strange sound he had heard earlier returned to his ears. Even the noise of the Winchesters could not dull its eerie music.

Were sirens of old calling out to him? Luring him to his death as they were reputed to have done to ancient mariners? Again Monrow turned in a vain attempt to outwit Cable's relentless bullets. Stride after painful stride Monrow persisted in what he now believed was a hopeless effort to escape the guns of his hunters.

The unearthly noise was getting louder. His mind tried to fathom what it was but he was too spent. Too damn spent.

He swayed like a man staggering from a saloon at midnight but continued to keep moving. Yet more shots rang out. Now their sound was deafening and told him that it was only a matter of time before they caught up with him.

How close were they?

A hundred yards?

Less?

They must have been firing in all directions, knowing that at least one of their number might find the man who was leaving the telltale tracks in the sand, Monrow thought. He was about to turn again but the bullets anticipated his endeavour. The sand around him was kicking up into his eyes as shots landed on all sides.

Time was running out.

Even half dead he was still able to figure that.

They had horses and he had two bleeding feet inside boots designed to slip into stirrups, not for running in. He was now only moments from certain death.

Time was running out.

In his confused mind he could actually envisage a massive hourglass suspended in the fog. Unlike the ocean of sand he was running upon, the sand in the imaginary glass vessel was almost gone. Bullets passed within inches of his head. He could feel his skin burning.

He forced himself on.

Monrow wondered if he should just stop and turn and start shooting back into the fog, but there was no time. Even to pause was to be riddled with their lead. The strange sound ahead of him seemed to have vanished for a moment. Had there even been a sound at all, he wondered?

Perhaps it had been the sound of his brain boiling inside his skull which he had heard. His eyes glanced up. The merciless sun was still beating its blinding rays down as it had done for hours.

Why didn't those riders aim their rifles up there? he asked himself. Shoot that damn sun out. Even if it only went out for a heartbeat it would be something.

The towering wall of fog moved like a massive group of tormenting ghosts before him. Monrow bowed his head and ran towards the mirage of the hourglass but it vanished like the water which had once filled the canteens he still carried.

The marshal no longer trusted anything he either heard or saw. For all he knew he might be dead already. Lying on the sand waiting for his body to rot enough to draw buzzards.

Suddenly the ground beneath his boots softened drastically and sent him staggering. A thought flashed through Monrow's tortured mind. Had he found quicksand? The way his luck was panning out, the young lawman knew it was possible.

If it was quicksand it might be preferable to the fate Cable and his henchmen had planned for him. He pressed on.

He felt the sand give way beneath his weight as he passed over it. It was in total contrast to all of the terrain of El Diablo he had so far encountered. His pace faltered. Now he was no longer running. Now Monrow was barely walking as the soft sand hampered his progress. He kept moving forward. He knew he had to try to get away from the shots which were again starting to close in on him.

Monrow looked over his shoulder back into the mist. It was impossible for any of them to see him, he thought. Not if he was unable to catch even a glimpse of them.

Two more strides.

Then the ground gave way completely.

He toppled forward helplessly. His arms began to flap like the wings of a buzzard trying to take to the air. But the young marshal was no bird. He was just a man who had somehow lost contact with the ground beneath his boots.

For a brief moment Monrow had no idea what was happening to him. He tried desperately to think. To consider. It was no use.

He was falling.

Falling down into a place he still could not see. It was like being swallowed alive by some invisible creature. He could do nothing but accept his fate.

More bullets carved their cruel way

through the mist which surrounded him. This time one of their number caught the falling man. He screamed in agony as he rotated in the air. A trail of bloody droplets curled in the acrid air around him like a necklace of rubies. He stared in disbelief at the hole in his pants leg just above his left knee.

A thin stream of blood was marking out his every twist and turn as he fell.

Monrow blinked hard as he found himself looking at his legs above him. If there was pain he could not feel it any longer. All he could do was fall.

And fall he did.

Monrow tried to look down but his body kept on rotating like a child's spinning top. There was no up or down any longer. Only the droplets of gore spewing from the bullet hole in his leg gave any clue to which way was up.

He screwed his eyes tight shut and awaited the impact he knew would more than likely kill him.

Was El Diablo devouring another innocent victim?

Rafe Monrow no longer gave a damn.

Somehow the border marshal hit the sloping sand with his boots first. Pain went through him like a well-aimed lightning bolt. Yet before he could scream out he felt his body tumbling head first. Monrow plunged for what felt like an eternity deeper into the chasm. Again he was helpless: little more than a limp puppet whose strings had been torn from his body. The only thing the lawman could be grateful for was that the ground he was tumbling down was soft. Dry sand flew up from every part of him as he cartwheeled ever downward.

It was like a dream. Or perhaps it was more like a satanic nightmare. El Diablo was toying with him as if he were little more than a rag doll being thrown away by some unseen giant child. Down and down he continued to fall. The sand was hotter the further down into the unknown he went. He could taste its heat in his open mouth as he vainly tried to scream.

Yet he no longer felt pain.

For to feel pain you have to be alive and Monrow had started to doubt that he were still in the land of the living. This was death. It had to be. This was being dragged down into the bowels of Hell itself and he knew it.

They say that when death is close your entire life flashes before you in the blinking of an eye.

Every small detail was kicking its way into the mind of the man who was bouncing off the deadly slope of blisteringly hot sand. Each moment of his short existence was being recalled in minute detail and what Monrow saw did not make him doubt he was headed in the right direction.

There would be no salvation for him.

Even though he wore a star and had tried to uphold the law for the years since the end of the war, he knew it made no difference.

For the war loomed in almost every corner of his mind.

The men he had killed were chanting at him from a heavenly place he knew he would never be allowed to reach.

It made no difference that he had been only doing what he had been ordered to do. He had slain his enemies willingly. Killed when maybe it might not have been required.

So many images flashed through his head as he continued to fall inexorably down into the foggy mist.

Each image as sickening as the last.

Then he felt the invisible mule kick him hard.

He had reached the bottom of the steep sandy mountain. The sudden impact had knocked every ounce of wind out of his body. He now felt the pain as it travelled throughout his entire length.

It had finally caught up with him.

Monrow lay on his face and chewed on the fine, hot granules his head had embedded itself in. He tried to force himself up but there was no strength in his arms any longer.

A burning anger festered above his knee. For the first time since the bullet had encountered his thigh he could feel the blood pumping out of the wound.

He managed to turn his face to one side and spit the sand from his mouth. His every sinew had been hot before but now he felt as if he were being roasted over a well-fed fire.

Sand filled his eyes and cut like glass. He could not see anything. Once more he tried to move but his limbs refused to obey his simple commands.

Then a chill overwhelmed him.

It defied the blazing heat which was cooking him.

The terrifying noise that had taunted Monrow for so very long had returned.

The only difference was that now it was closer.

Too close.

The bruised and bleeding marshal shook his head in a vain effort to shake the sand from his blinded eyes. Red-hot branding-irons could not have hurt more. It was no use, though. The sand remained embedded in his eyes and every part of his body was racked with pain. The noise mocked his dazed mind. He could not make out what he was listening to but whatever it was it was near his helpless outstretched form.

Somehow his aching fingers found the grip of his weapon. He was amazed that the Colt was still in his holster. His fingers toyed with the wooden grip but he could not drag it free. He was face down in the sand and it felt as though a buffalo was sitting on his back.

He coughed and tasted blood. The lawman then realized that he had bitten clean through his tongue on the violent fall down the steep slope.

The sound persisted.

What was it?

His brain was screaming out for answers. Answers he did not have. His head was hurting real bad now. It had never hurt like this before.

Monrow tried to rise up and face whatever was making the unearthly sound. Monrow summoned every scrap of his remaining energy and forced himself up.

Then everything fell into a black whirlpool. He felt as if he were being spun around by his ankles. Faster and faster he whirled until he could think no longer. He was falling again. This time he was falling into his own nightmares.

Monrow was no longer conscious.

11

Three days previously Rafe Monrow had not realized that even when surrounded by those who wanted him gone from their town he was probably safer than he would later find himself. Every shred of common sense told him to leave these people be, but that had never been his way. He had never run away from anything. Monrow had always faced his enemies square on. He had no idea what it meant to back down even when the odds were stacked against him.

The Black Heart saloon had looked like a thousand others but it was the people within its walls who made this drinking hole a lot different from all of its contemporaries. There had been death in their eyes and those eyes had all been aimed at the border marshal. If looks could kill then Monrow would have already been headed for Boot Hill.

It had been the longest five minutes Rafe Monrow had ever lived through. Amid so many hostile faces the beer had tasted like poison. His plan to try and gather some evidence to support his gut instincts had been fruitless. There had been barely a word spoken in the crowded Black Heart as he had rested a boot on the brass rail and leaned on the bar counter.

He had been able to smell the anger which had been brewing up in their hearts from the moment he had entered.

He was a star-packer. A real one, and that was something these folks had no liking for. He knew that he had stumbled innocently into the very place he had been ordered to find, but knowing something and actually proving it were two very different things. The good people of Panhandle seemed to have only one idea and that was to keep silent. They were not going to let the unwelcome visitor learn anything he could use to incriminate them.

No man had ever downed his two glasses of beer more swiftly than the young marshal had done. Again his smiles did not wash with any of the patrons of the saloon. He had left the Black Heart no wiser than when he had entered. Monrow returned to the street and wondered how long it would take them to start shooting. He paused on the boardwalk, eased his back against the wall and listened to the voices from inside the saloon wafting over the swing doors. Whatever they were saying was muffled by whispers.

The evening breeze did nothing to stem the beads of sweat which travelled down the length of his spine beneath his fresh shirt. Monrow had sensed that danger was all around him. Every shadow posed a threat to him.

And there were a lot of shadows in Panhandle.

The sky was dark but not black. There had been too many stars tussling with the moon for it to be truly dark but it was enough to make a man wary and Monrow was learning to be very wary.

He screwed up his eyes and glanced at the rooftops across the street. There seemed to be more rifles up there now. He swallowed hard as he counted them poking out from over the edges of the various flat-fronted façades.

His mind had drifted back to the people inside the saloon. He had tried to talk to them. It had been a waste of time. Even the whores had given him a wide berth, as though he were poison.

These people wanted only one thing.

His departure.

He began to wonder whether that meant dead or alive. They sure gave him the feeling that he might end up in the small cemetery at the side of the church if he did not watch his back.

A wiser, more seasoned man might have saddled his horse and headed out to try to find enough law officers to return with, because this was not a job for one man to tackle.

Not successfully anyway.

But Monrow had a failing that most men of his age have, and that was the impetuosity of youth. He, like so many who have yet to discover their first grey hair in their whiskers, think they are immortal.

After all, he had gone through a war without getting even a scratch along the way. Surely he had some guardian angel protecting his hide. Didn't he?

Monrow turned and walked along the boardwalk until he had reached the brightly lit office where he thought he might actually find another lawman.

That had been another false hope, for there was no one inside the sheriff's office except two men wearing tin stars. The deputy had not spoken or even acknowledged the entrance of the marshal as he oiled his arsenal of weaponry on his desk. The sheriff had not shown much more interest.

'Name's Monrow, Sheriff. Border Marshal.'

Sol Cannon had nodded slowly

before allowing his hooded eyes to stare up at the lean form before him. He adjusted his butt on the hard chair and began rolling a cigarette.

'Marshal.' He sighed.

'Just thought I'd come and tell ya why I'm here in Panhandle,' Monrow added.

'Ya looking for bandits.' Cannon exhaled as his fingers expertly rolled the paper until its gummed edge was facing his tongue. He licked the gum and then poked the smoke into the corner of his mouth. 'Wasting ya time.'

'And smugglers. I'm also looking for varmints who smuggle goods across the border.' Monrow looked down at the man who seemed little different from all of the other men in town.

'Ya gonna come up shy on both counts, boy.' The sheriff struck a match and then raised its flickering flame to the end of his cigarette. He inhaled, then blew the flame out.

'Ya reckon?'

'Yep.' Cannon leaned to his side and

spat a lump of black goo at the floor, which was already peppered with the tobacco stains of countless previous target practices. 'Nobody in this town fits that kinda varmint. We're all as honest as the day is long. Ya ought to get riding to the next town on ya map.'

Monrow rested his knuckles on the grip of his gun and stared down at the sheriff as smoke encircled Cannon's head.

'You telling me that there ain't no law-breaking in this town at all, Sheriff?' Monrow rested his wrist on the grip of his holstered weapon. There was something about both men which made him realize that either of them might start shooting at any moment. 'None at all?'

Again Cannon nodded. 'Yep. That's what I'm telling ya. Get riding and leave us law-abiding folks be. We don't cotton to folks that give us grief. Ride on out, Marshal.'

Monrow had been given a lot of advice in his time but this was not mere advice. This was a warning. A thinly veiled threat.

'A smart *hombre* would take heed,' the deputy piped up.

The marshal wandered back to the door and stared out into the street. He could see a man moving along the roof of the building opposite. He could also see the rifle in his hands. He tilted his head and stared hard into the eyes of Cannon as smoke drifted from the seated man's lips.

'How come ya got folks with carbines on the rooftops?'

'There ain't no law against it.' Cannon smiled.

'Why are they up there?'

Cannon eased his body out of his chair. 'Do they make ya a tad nervous, boy?'

'Nope,' Monrow answered. 'Just curious.'

'Ain't healthy to get curious. Not in these parts.'

The marshal inhaled. 'Folks keep telling me that.'

'Then heed them words, boy.' Cannon was smouldering as if he were a stick of dynamite with its fuse lit. 'Ain't even sure that ya knows where ya are. Panhandle might even be in Mexico for all we knows. There ain't no borders in these parts.'

'My map says it's in America,' Monrow said.

'Maps is nothing but paper, boy.' Cannon pointed a brown-stained finger at the younger man. 'Paper is darn fragile. It rips up and it burns. Only a fool places his faith in paper.'

Monrow knew that the deputy was watching his every move as though he were waiting for the nod from his superior to raise one of his weapons and let loose with a gutful of lead. The marshal gripped the brass doorknob and stared out into the strange amber light cast by the numerous streetlamps. His eyes then moved back to the man who was wearing the sheriff's star. A man whose head was encircled with smoke.

'What does Cable keep in that locked-up barn down yonder?'

Cannon smiled more widely. A sickly smile identical to the one Ford Cable had used on him earlier.

'That's his business.'

'Not if I make it mine.'

Cannon sighed. 'Ya just gotta keep gnawing at our craws, ain't ya?'

'That's what I'm paid to do.' Monrow pulled the door towards him. 'Where's the telegraph office?'

'Ain't got one of those, boy.' Cannon laughed.

'Figures.'

The two men watched as Monrow walked back out into the street. Their smiles evaporated as soon as he started along the boardwalk in the direction of the locked-up building.

'Git a scattergun,' Cannon snarled.

12

A million memories fought to take control of Monrow's mind as it spun into a place he had never been to before. Then through the clouds of pain he recalled the one thing which he wished he had managed to bury for ever. It was the deadly events which had led up to his long flight into El Diablo. Suddenly it was all as vivid as day. Every little detail came thundering into his head with crystalline clarity. No longer were they blurred into confused half-truths created by a merciless sun, a big thirst and horrific injuries.

Now Monrow saw it all as it had actually happened. Every last detail was being repeated in his mind as it fought against the blackness it had fallen into. Through the swirling mist inside his head Monrow saw the main street of Panhandle appear like a vision. This was no mirage where sand dunes become lakes of precious water. This was the dying embers of a dying man's mind as the last chapter of his life flashed before him.

It had been a studious Ford Cable who had scraped a match down the porch upright beside him and then raised it to the tip of the long cigar gripped between his teeth. The burly man inhaled slowly and savoured the smoke which filled his lungs. He tossed the match aside, then glanced across at the three rifle-toting men perched high above the street. They were watching and waiting for a signal as their leader stepped down into the street. Their eyes followed Cable as he walked towards the border marshal, who had been watching him as intently as he had been observing the lawman.

Lines of amber illumination spread across the dark sand between them as they closed in upon one another. Neither man slowed his pace.

Unable to ignore the building where

he suspected Cable had stored his ill-gotten gains for a moment longer, Monrow had once more aimed his boot leather at the heavily secured building set halfway along Main Street. The young marshal knew that it was probably the dumbest thing he had ever done, but Monrow had once been a pretty fair poker player. Now it was time to see if he could still bluff a man with a full house into folding against a pair of deuces.

Cable reached the large building a few seconds before the lawman and rested a boot on the edge of the boardwalk as Monrow slowed, then stopped a few feet away from him. Each man stared at the other.

'I want to take me a look inside that warehouse, Mr Cable.'

'I know that.' Cable grinned. The lantern light traced across the fine set of store-bought teeth that the older man sported.

'Ya gonna let me?' Monrow kept his wrist pressed down on the grip of his Colt as his fingers flexed above it.

'You seem to be under the impression that I've got goods inside that old barn, boy.' Cable sucked on the cigar. 'Goods I ain't meant to have.'

Monrow nodded firmly. 'Yep. That's what I reckon.'

Cable removed the cigar from his lips and tapped the ash away before returning it to his awaiting teeth. 'And ya want me to let ya go inside and take a looksee. Right?'

Monrow gave a slow nod. 'Yep.'

'I was afraid it would end up like this, Mr Monrow.' Cable sighed heavily. 'I was hoping that you might be a little bit smarter than the other nosy bastards wearing stars who have come to my town. But alas, ya ain't.'

'Sorry to disappoint ya.' The marshal suddenly noticed that there were others gathering in the street. Men with rifles and six-guns who were converging on them. For the first time since he had arrived in Panhandle Monrow knew that these folks meant business. 'So I'm not the first star-packer to ride into Panhandle. I won't be the last either.'

'We'll cross that bridge when we get to it, boy.' Cable drew in on the cigar. Its tip glowed red. 'Right now we've only one problem and you happen to be it.'

Monrow's eyes glanced around the wide girth of Cable at the other men. There were at least a dozen, with more appearing from every rat-infested alley. He felt his throat tighten as though a noose had been tightened around it. Now he heard them coming from behind him as well. He glanced at the windowpanes in the store-fronts and saw their reflections.

There had to be at least forty of them. All armed to the teeth and all with the same gruesome expressions carved in their features. Monrow exhaled and stared down at the ground at his feet. He wanted to run but knew that would be an open invitation for them to start shooting.

'What's going on, Cable?' The marshal asked through gritted teeth.

'How come ya vermin are showing their hand? If ya wanted me dead why have ya waited so long?'

'We were hoping that you might just take the hint and head on out of ya own accord,' Cable replied. 'But that was never really on the cards. Was it? Your kind just ain't smart enough to be dishonest.'

'I'm open to suggestions,' Monrow lied. 'Ya ain't even offered me anything yet.'

Cable smiled. 'Ya ain't much of a liar, are ya, boy? I've known your sort before. Plumb honest. We can't risk losing everything to someone who might bring the army down on us.'

'What you got in there?' Monrow whispered wryly.

Ford Cable stepped closer and blew a cloud of smoke into the lawman's face. He chuckled. 'Exactly what ya figured I got in there, Marshal. A fortune in Mexican silver and gold. Ready to be shipped north to make us at least eighty per cent profit.'

'Sweet,' Monrow acknowledged.

'Reckon it's time ya headed out.' Cable tapped ash from his smoke. 'Ya got an invite to El Diablo.'

'That where ya do all ya killing?'

'Yep.'

The sound of heavy boots on the boardwalk behind him drew Monrow's attention. His eyes saw both sheriff and deputy heading straight for him with primed scatterguns cradled like babies in their hands. A cold chill swept down his spine as he realized that he had played his hand badly. Now there seemed to be no way out of this.

Monrow knew he ought to fold, but that had never been his way.

Something had to turn up to save his bacon. All he had to do was be alert enough to spot his chance and grab it firmly with both hands.

The marshal returned his full attention to Cable, who was now less than two feet from him. Again he glanced through the murky half-light of a thousand stars and coal-tar lanterns.

Every face was screwed up in determined resolve. They wanted him dead and all he had to do was try and disappoint them.

'Ya got yourself a mighty big troop of men, Cable,' Monrow noted as his brain tried to think of a way out of the cesspool he had wandered into.

Cable frowned. 'This ain't but a few of the gunmen who do as I tell them, boy.'

'Oh.' A thoughtful Monrow nodded; then, faster than the blink of an eye, he reached out and dragged Cable's Remington from its holster, cocked its hammer and pushed its cold steel between the large man's eyes and shouted. 'One more step and I'll send Mr Cable to meet his Maker, boys.'

Every man in the street stopped advancing.

Monrow grabbed Cable's collar and pulled him close enough to smell his fresh pomade. 'Call 'em off, Cable. Call 'em off or I'll surely kill you. I ain't got nothing to lose.'

The smile had vanished from Cable's face the moment he felt the cold metal pressing into his temple. Now it had been replaced by a grim glare. 'Ya bluffing, Marshal. That would be illegal and I don't figure on your sort ever breaking no laws. Admit it, it ain't ya way.'

'Bluffing?' Monrow pushed the barrel harder into his defiant captive's brow. Ford Cable winced in pain. 'Call 'em off right now or I'll happily settle for being covered in ya brain juice. Do you hear me, fat old man? Call 'em off.'

'I hear ya, Monrow,' Cable snarled as he waved a hand at his troop of gunmen. 'Drop them guns and back off. This star-packer is rattled enough to blow my head clean off if'n ya don't.'

Sol Cannon took a step forward and ran the palm of his left hand along the barrel of his twin-barrelled scattergun. 'But he's gotta be killed, Ford. We gotta finish him just like ya told us earlier. He knows too much. We can't just let the varmint go. He'll bring the army down on us. It'll be the ruin of Panhandle.'

'Do as I tell ya,' Cable screamed out.

Bo Fontaine pushed his way through the wall of men until he was within twenty feet of both Monrow and Cable. His mane of white hair hung over his angry eyes. He was nursing his .45 in eagerness to start firing. 'I can kill that young star-packer with one shot, Ford. I can take his head clean off before he got time to squeeze his trigger.'

Cable's eyes darted to Fontaine. Beads of sweat started to roll down his face from his hatband to where the barrel of Monrow's weapon was pressed into his flesh.

'Are ya loco? One twitch of this bastard's finger and it'll be my head that gets blown off, not his. He's got my Remington here and its got the hairiest trigger in town,' Cable ranted loudly. 'Drop ya damn guns and get the hell out of here. Savvy?'

A disappointed growl washed round the crowd of gunmen. They were like a pack of hounds that could see the fox.

Rafe Monrow pressed his mouth against Cable's ear and whispered, 'I figure we both just might live a tad longer. Either that or we'll be on our way to hell damn soon.'

'I'll kill ya myself when this is over, Monrow. I promise ya that,' Cable snarled from the corner of his mouth as the younger man turned him around like a shield.

'The way it looks right now it's even odds we both get shot before too long.' Monrow pushed his human shield forward towards the smallest group of stationary figures.

'Drop them guns, ya fools,' Cable yelled out.

Reluctantly one by one the men did as they were ordered and dropped their six-shooters and Winchesters on to the ground.

'Back off,' Monrow shouted at the top of his voice. Cannon and the deputy eased their way backwards as the lawman and his hostage drew ever closer to them. 'Drop them scatterguns. Now.'

Suddenly Brody Barr burst through the crowd with an ancient seven-inch-barrelled Colt clutched in his shaking hands. A gasp of horror spread through the men who surrounded the nervous marshal and his captive.

'Don't ya go fretting none, Ford,' Barr yelled out at the top of his voice as he levelled the gun at Monrow. 'He'll not get out of Panhandle to spread the word.'

Before anyone could utter a solitary word the gun erupted into action. A red flame spewed from the long barrel and tore through the air towards the two men standing in the centre of the main street.

Monrow released his grip as the bullet tore Cable's hat off his head, leaving a bloody track across his scalp in its wake. Cable stumbled and fell to his knees as a line of blood ran down his head from the burning graze.

'Ya damn fool,' Cable growled, holding the palm of his left hand over the graze.

Monrow was standing alone. He swung full circle and fanned the hammer of his Colt. Barr was plucked off his feet and dropped at the boot leather of Fontaine. Every eye stared at the smoking hole in the head of the dead man.

'Get him,' a dozen voices called out together. Hands reached down to get their weaponry off the sand.

Flames of fiery lead spewed at Monrow from all directions as one man after another retrieved his gun. The border marshal turned on his heels and ran for all he was worth to the nearest alleyway as bullets erupted from countless gun and rifle barrels. Shards of wood were blasted off porch uprights as the young man headed for the nearest shadow. Monrow threw himself over a water trough as the lethal lead tore into its wooden form. Fountains of water rose up into the lantern light as one shot after another found the trough.

As he had learned to do during the war, Monrow cocked the hammer of his Colt and blasted shots back at the crowd in quick succession. He heard them scatter for their own cover and briefly the gunplay paused. That was all he required.

Like a mountain lion the young starpacker scrambled away from his wooden shield and ran towards a narrow gap between two buildings. As he ran he expertly shook the spent shells from his weapon and reloaded his smoking gun. He kept on running until he reached the very end of the narrow alley. There were high fences on both sides, which continued into darkness. In one fluid action he stepped up on a barrel and leapt over the fence to his right. He landed in the back yard of the café. He could tell that by the scent of cooking coming from the open rear door.

For a few endless seconds Monrow just stood holding his smoking gun in the shadows as he listened to the sound of angry men running down the alley in pursuit of their prey.

The female who had stared at him without a hint of emotion whilst he had eaten his supper stepped out into the yard as though drawn by the sound of the hunting men.

Monrow stared straight at her. Their eyes burned into each other's souls.

For the first time she looked as though she were going to open that mouth of hers. She inhaled and was about to scream out to alert the men to the lawman's whereabouts.

Again Monrow sprang like a puma. This time right at her. He knew he had to silence her if he were to have any chance of escaping the gunmen. He holstered his Colt and grabbed her with both hands. Her stunned expression was that of a woman who had not been manhandled for an awful long while.

Monrow clenched his fist.

He struck her with a blow which could have knocked a prize fighter out, but he did not care. She had to be silenced. The sound of her teeth shattering fell on deaf ears.

She dropped at his feet like a felled tree.

Without a moment's hesitation Monrow stepped over her and moved swiftly through the kitchen towards the café he had visited only half an hour earlier. His plate and cup were still on the table where he had left them.

He had extinguished every lamp inside the room before he reached the door and its lowered blind. With his heart pounding like a drum inside his chest Monrow rested a shoulder against the door-frame and teased the blind away from the glass.

Monrow was sweating now. His shirt-back was soaked as fear filled his every sinew. His narrowed eyes stared out into the well-lit street and studied the scene. There were still half a dozen of Cable's men there. They had helped their sturdy leader back to his feet whilst the others searched for Monrow. The sound of shots being fired around the town told Monrow that they were killing a lot of shadows in their craving for his hide.

Then he heard another noise. His

eyes looked up as two men clattered on to the roof of the porch above the café, then dropped down on to the sand. Both riflemen ran to Cable.

'The roof,' Monrow said to himself. 'That's it. They're looking for a man on the ground. Not another man up on the rooftops.'

The border marshal turned and ran back into the kitchen where he had passed a staircase after knocking the female out. He grabbed the rail and mounted the steps two at a time until he reached a landing. He entered the first bedroom he came to and made his way to the window at the front of the building. It looked out on to the porch and the main street.

Monrow holstered his .45 and unlocked the window latch. He eased it up, then followed his long left leg out into the darkness. He crouched behind the café façade. He looked up at the roof. It was only about eight feet to the flat roof.

Cable led the men who had encircled

him to the alley. Monrow tilted his head and stared across the wide street to the roofs opposite him. The riflemen there were beginning to descend from their lofty perches.

Monrow glanced to his left.

That was where the livery stable was, and his trusty horse. He had instructed the old-timer there to make his horse ready for eight o'clock. He wondered what the time was. It would be certain that some of those men who were hunting him would eventually head for the stable and wait for him. The lawman knew he had to cause a diversion.

Something which might buy him time to reach the stable and his waiting horse.

Then his eyes beheld the answer.

The neatly painted sign on the whorehouse was easily seen from his high vantage point. Two oil-filled lanterns screwed to the front wall cast their amber light all over it and the scarlet doorframe below.

Monrow cocked the hammer of his Colt, and then rested his outstretched arm on the rail before him. He closed one eye and aimed at one of the lanterns. His finger eased back and caressed the trigger the way men were probably caressing the painted doves inside the building.

He fired.

The nearer of the lanterns shattered as the bullet passed through its oil bowl. As the oil poured down on to the boardwalk it erupted into flame. It spread like a cancer. Suddenly the whole front of the whorehouse was ablaze. Females began to scream from inside the building.

Men appeared from everywhere and rushed to the inferno.

Even the men who had been hunting him appeared from the side streets and lanes below where he knelt and were also drawn to the building's burning front as choking smoke billowed out into the thoroughfare. Even Ford Cable ran towards it.

'That oughta keep them busy for a while,' Monrow said as he watched them swarm to the building. Again with the agility of a cat Monrow turned and clambered upwards. It took him less than half a minute to reach the flat, shingled roof of the café. He ran across it and jumped to the next roof.

There was no time to lose.

Monrow knew that even a burning whorehouse would not distract these men for long. Soon they would figure out what was happening. He had to reach his horse and head out of town as fast as the black gelding would take him.

As the young man leapt to another roof he realized that he did not have as much time as he had hoped for. The air lit up with rods of deadly venom as rifle shots cut through the night air after him.

Ducking the fearsome lead he bent his knees and dropped to a balcony below him. Then he swung over the rail and fell to earth.

13

The dark alley suddenly became illuminated with short bursts of deadly lead as Cable's followers let loose with their arsenal of weaponry. Bullets came from everywhere as they sought out the border marshal. The air was burning as a million splinters were torn from the wooden walls which surrounded Monrow. The narrow confines lit up as each of the red-hot tapers of death flew like rods of lightning into its heart. All the lawman could do was wait until one or all of them had to pause and reload. Monrow remained kneeling as chunks of wood were torn from the wall less than six feet before him. Choking smoke filled the length of the alley. It wrapped around him like a blanket. A nervous soul might have been ready to quit, but not Monrow. He just gritted his teeth and waited. He knew there was no profit in being scared. Not now. It was too late for that pointless emotion.

Hoping to keep his pursuers at a distance, Monrow fanned his hammer and fired to either side in quick succession. Then he shook the hot casings from his .45 and hastily filled the smoking chambers with fresh bullets from his belt.

He rubbed his knees. They hurt.

He had dropped over twelve feet from the balcony above him into the dark lane, but a dozen or more bullets had followed him from the unseen rifles every inch of the way. Now he could taste the gunsmoke lingering on the night air. It was an acrid flavour that he knew all too well.

As more smoke filled the alley and mingled with the shadows Monrow realized that his attackers could no longer see their chosen target. Now he was invisible.

Totally invisible.

He sprang to his full height and clawed back on the hammer of his Colt until his ears heard the distinctive clicking of its locking into position. He was ready to kill if they wanted it that way. There were no more doubts in his young mind. The last few minutes had made it clear that he was a dead man if he did not escape from Panhandle. He was not ready to die alone.

He was gasping for air. Trying desperately to fill his lungs with enough air to get him over the last hurdle that stood before him. His head turned one way and then the other. His eyes stared down the alley.

Shots began again. The planks of wood of the house in front of him again shattered as lead hit it from both sides.

Unlike the majority of premises facing the main street the building in front of him was just an ordinary house. It had a sash window set midway along its front wall. Pressing his back against the porch upright Monrow holstered his gun and raised his arms until they covered his face. He rocked back and forth for a few seconds, then ran straight at the two-foot-square window.

He leapt straight at it and crashed straight through its weathered frame. Glass shattered and followed him into the interior of the house. He hit the floor and rolled across its boarded flooring until an internal wall brought him to an abrupt halt.

The lawman got carefully to his feet and felt the sting of glass in his arms. He shook himself and listened as the glass landed at his feet. Again the shooting outside seemed to pause as his hunters started to close in on the alley and their prey.

There was no time to lose. He had to get out of here and continue on his way towards the stables. He knew there was only one more building between himself and his goal. One more building and he would reach the black gelding; he prayed it had been saddled as he had instructed.

Monrow turned, screwed up his eyes and tried to make out the layout of the small house. The interior was dark.

Whoever lived here was out. Probably hunting him with the rest of the pack, he concluded.

The only light came in through the broken window frame through which he had crashed. Eerie shafts of amber lantern light traced through the dusty air.

Once more he listened.

The crowd seemed to be getting louder with every beat of his heart. They could sense that they were closing in on the weary star-packer. They could already taste his blood in their rabid mouths.

Monrow was about to move when his holster caught something at his side. His hands reached out and found an ornate lamp on a solidly-built table.

He lifted the glass lamp and shook it. The sound of the liquid told Monrow that its bowl was full of oil. His head turned and he heard the men outside. They were at both ends of the alley, waiting for the gunsmoke to lift.

Quickly Monrow removed the glass

funnel from the lamp and placed it on the table. Then he unscrewed the brass fitting and its wick. He held the bowl and walked across the broken glass to the broken window and began to pour the oil over the frame so that it soaked the outside wall. He then made his way through the house, leaving a trail of oil in his wake on the boarded flooring.

He reached another window on the far side of the house. He placed the bowl down, then slid the window upward until it was fully open. Silently he eased his long lean body out into another narrow lane.

The shooting and shouting resumed on the opposite side of the little house from which he had just emerged. Once more he knew he had to create a distraction. Something to gain him a few precious seconds so that he could get to his waiting horse. Monrow slid fingers and thumb into his pants pocket. He pulled out a box of matches and removed one of them. His thumb-nail ignited the lucifer into flame.

Monrow held his hand inside the window and dropped the burning match on to the oil-filled lamp bowl.

A mighty burst of heat and light erupted as the oil turned into deathly flames. Suddenly the house was filled with flames which ran across the trail of oil back to the alley on the opposite side of the house. The entire endeavour had taken a matter of mere seconds. He hoped it might buy him an equal amount of time. Time he needed to escape.

Black smoke billowed out from the open window. Monrow heard the shocked yells of the man-hunters, then he took to his heels and ran.

The building between himself and the livery stable was a hardware store. Unlike most of the other premises along Main Street it had a pitched roof of wooden shingles. Yet even that did not deter the lawman. He reached the back wall, mounted a fence and threw himself at the wall. Using his gloved fingers and pointed toecaps Monrow clambered up towards the end of the roof overhang with the agility of a man half his age.

It took every scrap of his strength and resolve to swing his long lean frame up on to the edge of the shingles. Some were dislodged and fell into the rear yard of the hardware store, but Monrow paid no heed. He got himself up on to his feet and started to walk across the shingles towards the big livery stable that stood eight feet from the roof overhang.

As Monrow reached the very end of the roof he heard it groan beneath his boots. He paused when he felt the edge of the roof give under his weight. Cautiously the marshal stepped back. He stared across at the dark livery building, rubbed a knuckle across his chin and pondered the problem.

He knew he had to get across that eight-foot gap. That meant he either went back down to the ground or he jumped. Neither option looked attractive. He carefully made his way up the sloping roof towards the highest point of the hardware store as flames and black smoke burned through the roof of the house next door. Like living creatures the flames curled and danced into the sky. Monrow could hear other lamps exploding inside the house as the fire grew more intense.

He turned away from the sight of the fire and concentrated on the problem in hand. He rested on the very top of the roof. Even perched on the highest part of the hardware store he had to look up to see the top of the livery.

He had leapt more than eight feet many times in his life, but from the roof of a building dwarfed by another the distance seemed to be growing. Monrow eased his position and looked down. He felt his throat tighten as it became obvious that to fall from this height could be a tad fatal.

There had to be a way of bridging that gap, his mind had kept telling him.

There just had to be. His black gelding was waiting to carry him away from this cursed town. All he had to do was get to the damn thing.

He eased himself down on to one knee and held on to the top of the roof with one hand whilst the other remained close to his gun grip. A lot of men were running around shooting at shadows far below him, whilst others were hauling buckets through water troughs and trying to put out the fires which the lawman had started. Clouds of acrid smoke swept through the town as the fires consumed more and more dry wood.

Monrow turned his head and peered over the roof. The whorehouse was well ablaze at the other end of main street. The house where he had set match to oil was now engulfed in scarlet fury. The cruel twisting flames were consuming its weathered dry walls faster than Monrow had imagined possible. Like the desert which surrounded Panhandle this settlement was tinder dry.

He heard the men in the lane between the hardware store and the stables pass below him. The star-packer watched them as they were drawn to the new fire.

Most of them were occupied by his handiwork. Most but by no means all. The rifle-toting men were still searching. They would not stop until they had his head on a pike.

Suddenly he noticed that the alley below him was empty.

Monrow glanced up at the higher building and swallowed hard. It was now or never, he told himself. He stood up, balanced as best he could and stared at the building he intended to try and reach with one heroic leap.

Then he saw something which the shadows and smoke had hidden from him until this very moment.

He stared at the wooden ladder nailed to the stable wall. It went from the ground and stopped next to a hayloft door. The door was partly open beneath a chain and pulley.

Taking his courage in his hands the marshal walked back eight paces, then paused. This was not going to be easy with one leg lower than the other. Summoning every scrap of his courage he inhaled deeply, then ran across the shingles. He kept staring at the ladder, the few inches of gap between the hayloft door and the rest of the massive wall.

There was no time to hesitate now. No time to stop. Monrow reached the edge of the shingled roof and jumped.

Men were not meant to be able to fly but Rafe Monrow somehow defied every rule by which he had lived his life and did just that: he flew the distance between the roof of the hardware store and the side wall of the livery stable. Faster than he had anticipated the marshal reached his goal. He clattered into the dark wooden wall and felt himself falling. Desperately Monrow grabbed hold of the rungs of the ladder just in time. He felt himself swinging helplessly like a clock pendulum until his boots touched the ladder rungs.

The marshal stretched out his left

hand and pulled the hayloft door open, then he clutched its frame. He dragged himself into the loft and fell to his knees. Regaining his wind he crawled over bales of dry hay until he had reached the edge of the platform. The familiar aroma of horses filled his flared nostrils. Monrow lay on his belly and looked down into the heart of the stable. There were a dozen or more horses in stalls. Some of the animals seemed to sense that there was an unexpected intruder high above them.

A blacksmith's forge glowed in the corner of the stable, casting a crimson light around the place. Monrow saw a shadow moving towards the centre of the stables. He leaned over the wooden parapet and squinted down. It was the liveryman whom he had entrusted with looking after his mount hours earlier. The man was leading the marshal's black gelding away from a stall. It was saddled, just as Monrow had requested.

The young lawman rose to his feet and moved to a ladder secured to the edge of the platform. Holding on to the uprights he began to make his way down. Monrow descended fast.

There was a look of utter surprise on the face of the old-timer as Monrow reached the ground and hastily made his way towards him.

'Where in tarnation have you bin hiding, sonny?' the liveryman asked as Monrow took the reins from his hands and tossed them over the head and neck of his trusty horse. 'What was ya doing up there in my loft?'

'It's a long story, friend.' Monrow handed a few coins to the man, stepped into his stirrup and mounted his horse. 'I'm kinda surprised that you ain't started shooting at me like the rest of the men in Panhandle.'

'I figured they'd start shooting at that star of yours sooner or later,' the old-timer said.

'Sure wish that you'd warned me.' Monrow gathered up his reins and swallowed hard.

The man scratched the side of his

whiskered jaw and looked up at Monrow. 'Ya looks kinda troubled.'

'I surely am.' Monrow turned the animal until it was facing the half-closed double doors of the livery. 'I never had to duck so many damn bullets in all my life.'

The old man walked beside the gelding's shoulder as Monrow approached the door. 'Smells like there's a fire some-place close.'

'There is.' Monrow shrugged as he stood in his stirrups and leaned beyond the doors. 'A couple of them.'

The old man rested a bony hand on his hip and looked hard at the marshal. 'I don't cotton to what's bin going on in this town for the last few years, sonny. Ever since Ford Cable got himself an itch to be wealthy the whole town has bin scratching mighty hard.'

'So you ain't one of the folks who like shooting at star-packers?' Monrow said, his eyes searching the street for further trouble.

'Nope. I don't like killing.' The old-timer sniffed at the smoke-filled air.

'Smells like the whole town is burning.'

'Sure does.' Monrow could feel his heart pounding. He could not see anyone close to the livery but that did not mean that some of the riflemen were not close.

'They don't cotton to star-packers in Panhandle,' the liveryman remarked. 'It kinda cramps their style, if'n ya gets my drift?'

'I kinda found that out the hard way.' Monrow nodded, gently tapped his spurs and nudged the horse to make its way out into the lantern-lit side street. Clouds of acrid smoke drifted across the barren area. The liveryman had remained at the horse's shoulder each step of the way.

'If I was you I'd spur that nag hard and long, sonny. This surely ain't the healthiest place to visit.' The old man sighed.

Monrow looked around at his saddle-bags. He knew they had barely enough provisions to last more than a few days. He lifted his pair of canteens. They had been refilled by the whiskered old-timer. 'Thanks for filling up my — '

There was no time to finish the sentence. Suddenly shots rang out as loudly as the church bell had done when announcing the arrival of the marshal to the strange town. Both bullets tore into the wall of the livery above Monrow's head. The marshal steadied his horse with one hand and dragged his Winchester from its scabbard with the other. In one well-rehearsed action Monrow spun the rifle around until its magazine was primed.

'Take cover,' Monrow shouted at the old man as he squinted and saw them. There were half a dozen riflemen running towards him. All with their Winchesters firing. Monrow raised his own rifle to his shoulder, looked along its barrel and teased back on its trigger. He sent a bullet straight into the closest of the men. He cranked the hand guard down, then fired again. The lawman winged another of his attackers and sent him hobbling for cover.

'I'd get out of here, sonny,' the liveryman shouted out from the side of the large open door as bullets tore through its weathered slats.

'Good thinking,' Monrow shouted back. He turned his horse and then felt a bullet hitting his rifle stock. The entire weapon was torn from his hand by the impact. Holding his reins with his left hand Monrow drew his Colt and started to fire at his hunters. He saw three of them buckle before he drove his spurs into the flesh of his faithful mount.

The muscular horse obeyed.

The gelding thundered away from the gunplay.

Monrow spurred again.

The black horse galloped across the side street and turned into a lane. Its hoofs ate up the ground, sending dust up into the air.

An eerie sound of galloping hoofs echoed through the town as the lawman made his desperate attempt to escape the fury of those who wanted only one thing: his immediate death.

The horse thundered on as its master kept firing back at the men who were shooting at him. At last their bullets ceased to trail his flight.

The young lawman had chosen one of only three trails out of Panhandle. The problem was that he had chosen the wrong one.

As Monrow feverishly spurred into a high-shouldered canyon he had no idea that he was heading straight into the remorseless desert.

Monrow was blindly riding not to safety but straight into the bowels of Hell itself and the jaws of death. It would only become obvious when the sun rose and he suddenly realized that he was not riding north but south. And south led to only one place. A place to be avoided at all costs.

The very place to which Ford Cable and his cronies had taken previous lawmen to dispose of them. The place created by the Devil himself.

El Diablo.

14

The mist still lingered a couple of feet above the arid white-hot sand as the line of weary horsemen followed the tracks left by the fleeing Monrow. The riders had reached the very spot where their prey had fallen. The churned-up sand told the story to anyone with eyes capable of seeing. It was obvious that the sand had given way beneath Monrow and he had fallen helplessly down into the swirling soup of fog which rose from the deep canyon.

Ford Cable was the first to drag his reins up to his chest and stop his powerful horse. His fellow man-hunters all copied their leader even though none of them had noticed the deathly precipice. Suddenly their voices all blended into one as they realized that if their horses had gone forward another five feet they too would have fallen into the fathomless pit.

Fontaine leapt from his saddle and cautiously edged close to the sudden and brutal drop. A drop which appeared to be the kind that did not take prisoners.

'Holy Mother. Anyone falling off here must be a goner, Ford,' the silver-haired man announced as he mopped the sweat off his brow with a sleeve. 'That star-packer must be dead. That's gotta be hundreds of feet deep. I can't see the bottom.'

Cable listened to the words but did not believe that Monrow would be so easily killed. He had wasted three days trying and not managed the feat. 'Ain't certain he's dead, Bo. Gotta be certain if'n we're not to have the army brought in on us.'

Sol Cannon had also dismounted. He walked in front of the line of horses and stared at the sand, which grew softer the closer a man ventured to the rim of the sudden drop. He paused and looked hard at the boot tracks which led to the spot right in front of Cable's horse. A large chunk of sand was missing where the ground had swallowed up the naíve lawman. 'Bo's right. Look at the sand. It done gave way right in front of that marshal's boot markings. The ground give way right under him and there ain't no sign he managed to stop himself from falling. If'n he'd managed to scramble clear there'd be signs. Ain't no signs. He gotta be dead. Dead as a turkey on the fourth of July.'

Cable was still not convinced. 'I want to see his body with my own eyes. I want to make sure he is dead before I'll ever believe it.'

'But no man could fall all the way down there and live, Ford,' Fontaine protested, waving an arm. 'Ain't possible. That's a neck-break fall if'n I ever seen one.'

'Ya might be right, Bo.' Cable shrugged. 'But I want to be sure. How else can we carry on with our business if we don't know he's dead for sure?'

'We don't have to see his stinking carcass to know he's dead, Ford.'

Cannon ambled back along the line of snorting horses, grabbed his reins and mounted his buckskin once more.

'I do,' Cable growled.

'That's locobean talk and ya knows it,' another of their number piped up along the line of riders.

'Nobody could survive that kinda fall,' Fontaine noted as he tried to see the bottom of the canyon and failed. 'That marshal must have broke every damn bone in his body on the way down there.'

Cable was staring intently at the boot tracks which led up to the rim of the chasm. 'That bastard should have bin dead three days back in Panhandle. But he got this far. That *hombre* is lucky. Ya can't bet against a critter with that kind of luck on his side. We have to make sure he is dead like the others or there's a chance he'll make his way back to tell on us. We can't risk it.'

'Ya sound scared, Ford,' Fontaine said. He held on to his saddle horn and poked a boot into a stirrup. 'I never

155

seen ya scared of no lawman before.'

'I ain't scared,' Cable snarled. 'I'm wary. A man has call to be wary when he can't see another man's cards. That marshal got the better of us back in town. We had him and he got away. Burned down half the town in the process. Nope, that bastard ain't ya normal type of star-packer. He got himself a whole wagonload of luck on his side. We have to make sure that luck has run out.'

Suddenly, for no apparent reason, the ears of their horses pricked up and the mounts all shied away from the edge of the steep drop. The horsemen were baffled, then they also heard the strange, haunting sound: a sound which had been riding with them just as it had done with Monrow.

'There it is again,' Cannon said. 'Ya hear it?'

'I hear it,' Cable snapped as he tried to fathom what was making such an odd noise out here in the heart of El Diablo.

Fontaine moved his mount closer to Cable's. 'What ya figure that is, Ford?'

'Whatever it is it's coming up from down there.' Cable pointed a finger into the mist-filled chasm.

'Ghosts,' a voice said from along the line. 'Ghosts of them lawmen we done for.'

'Sounds kinda like bells to me,' the rider with the deputy star ventured nervously.

'Ain't nothing like bells,' Cable shouted angrily.

'And I don't believe in ghosts.'

'Then what is it?' Fontaine stammered.

'It sure got these nags spooked.' Cannon gulped.

Cable swung his horse around, narrowed his eyes and looked to their right. He raised a finger and pointed. 'About two miles down thataway is a draw which leads down into what's gotta be the start of this chasm. I seen it last time we was out here, disposing of a lawman. I figure we ought to head on down there and then we'll be able to kill two birds with one stone.'

'Come again?' Fontaine screwed up his eyes and stared at the sturdy Cable.

Cannon gripped his reins tightly. 'It does sound a little like ghosts wailing.'

Ford Cable gritted his teeth. 'We'll be able to find out what's making that infernal noise and we'll also get to find out if'n that star-packer is either dead or alive. C'mon.'

The leader of the riders spurred and rode off in the direction he had indicated to the others.

Reluctantly the rest of the jittery horsemen followed.

15

The sky was no longer aflame. The sun had started upon its descent towards the horizon where it would disappear until another dawn. Dust curled up off the hoofs of the band of horsemen who trailed their leader down into the draw. The heavens had begun to glow like embers in the cloudless sky above them. Soon it would darken and then a thousand stars would start to sparkle. This was further than any of them had ever ventured into El Diablo. Further than any sane man would willingly go.

Not unless there was a burning question to be answered. One that was gnawing at the craw of the man who led them.

Ford Cable was driven by only one question and that was a mighty important one. Had the border marshal finally died or was he somehow still alive?

Cable was a man who knew that his entire life could come crumbling down around his ears just like the ashes they had left behind in Panhandle. He knew that the youthful Monrow was more than capable of destroying the lucrative life he and his fellow riders had created for themselves.

Cable simply could not allow that to happen. He was a man who had grown rich by breaking the law at every opportunity that had presented itself. Now he knew that the only sure way to remain one step ahead of those who imposed those laws was to make sure that the border marshal was really dead.

Cable had to find the corpse. Shake it until he was convinced it was truly dead. Then put a bullet between Monrow's eyes to make doubly sure. Anything less was to risk everything he and the others had made for themselves.

He drove his exhausted mount on.

They kept following the steep downward trail until at last they found themselves at the opening of the chasm. As they faced into it they felt an unexpected cool breeze hit them. It was being channelled along the length of the crevasse from some unknown source. Suddenly they had something besides dust to suck into their burning lungs. Cool sweet air.

They drew rein and stopped their horses. None of them knew that the crevasse in the otherwise almost featureless terrain had been created thousands of years earlier, when rivers had flowed through this now parched landscape. There was little evidence now of the long-lost water-ways. The steep sandstone slopes to both sides of the line of horsemen loomed over them like giants.

The mist which had dogged their hunt for days seemed to be lifting as the breeze stiffened its resolve.

Cable stood in his stirrups and glared around them at the arid scene. Whatever lay ahead beyond the wall of fog was still hidden from their reddened eyes.

'I don't like it one bit, Ford,' Fontaine said frankly, as he fought to keep his mount steady. 'We're low on water and provisions. We've come too far.'

'Listen up,' Cable interrupted.

They all listened.

It was the eerie sound again. Now it seemed to be almost within spitting distance from the spot where their horses were champing on their bits.

'I still reckon that sounds like ghosts,' Cannon said as he felt his heart quicken its pace inside his chest. 'I'm for heading back. Who gives a damn what's down yonder anyways?'

'Ya yella,' Cable spat. 'Plumb yella.'

'Better to be yella than dead,' Cannon grunted. 'It don't make no sense at all for us to ride into there.'

Cable lowered his ample rump back on to his saddle and thought for a few moments. Whatever was making that noise had to be close. 'I ain't scared of no damn noise.'

Fontaine looked at the rest of their bunch and the lathered-up horses. He

162

leaned across to Cable.

'We oughta water and grain the horses, Ford,' he suggested as a way to delay their ride into the chasm. 'We could rustle up some vittles for us as well.'

Cable's eyes darted at Fontaine. 'Ya just like the rest of this herd of cowards, Bo. Ya want to hightail it and not find out the answers to our questions.'

'That ain't fair, Ford,' Fontaine protested. 'I've always stuck to ya like a pal. But I'm a tad nervous of what we might find out there. Besides it'll be dark in an hour or so.'

'Exactly. It'll be dark soon.' Cable pointed straight ahead to where the noise seemed to be coming from. 'I don't wanna waste another night bedded down in this desert. We head on up there to see if that marshal is truly dead. Then, when we knows the answer we can turn back for home. I don't wanna bed down one more night in this hell.'

Fontaine shrugged. He had lost his desire to argue. A simple nod was all that he could muster.

Cable pulled his long rifle from its scabbard and began to force bullets into its magazine. As each bullet was slid into the Winchester he looked at his frightened followers. 'We might be heading back home in a hour or less. Once we find that stinking Monrow's body we can turn tail for Panhandle. Now load them rifles and let's ride. I figure we'll find his body less than a couple of miles or so from here.'

'What we gonna do when we do find it?' Cannon asked.

A smiling Cable stared at his men and slowly replied: 'Burn his filthy carcass. Burn it like he burned up Panhandle.'

The riders did as they had been ordered. They made sure that carbines were fully loaded, then rested them across the horns of their saddles and waited for Cable to raise his arm.

'C'mon, boys. We got us a body to up and kill.'

The line of horses were encouraged to walk towards the breeze by their masters. But only Cable himself seemed to want to rush into the unknown.

Eventually they all spurred and galloped towards the wall of fog which masked the chasm from their curious eyes.

The mysterious noise grew louder.

16

The swirling fog of delirium evaporated at last into the sand beneath Monrow's sun-blistered face. The distant sound of horses' hoofs beating into the floor of the chasm resounded inside his head. It was enough to drag him back from the crystal-clear memories into the brutal reality of his painful situation. The previous three days were gone. Now there was only the present. The bloody present.

The injured border marshal coughed himself back to total consciousness. There was no way of knowing how long he had been lying in a crumpled heap at the foot of the great wall of sand down which he had cascaded. All there was, was the knowledge that the hoof-beats were warning him that his worst fears might soon be realized. Cable was still coming. Still coming with his small army of riflemen to finish him off. Monrow knew that the memories that had haunted him since he had fled into El Diablo were now gone. They had reached their conclusion. Whatever was left of his life now lay ahead and not behind him.

Suddenly Monrow realized that he was still alive. Against all the odds he was still somehow alive. He had to be alive because every small movement sent agonizing bolts of unimaginable pain coursing through him.

Dead men felt no pain.

Only the living felt pain.

He managed to move his hands and then both arms until they found his bloodied face. He rubbed the sand from his eyes until eventually he was able to see once more. It was like looking through a dirty pane of glass, but it was sight.

A breeze caught him. It felt good. He glanced up and noticed that the sky was getting darker with every beat of his pounding heart. At last the damn sun was setting, he thought. That meant a few hours of relief from its merciless heat.

Then he remembered the riders who were approaching. The palm of his left hand was pressed on to the sand. He could still feel the hoofs as the riders' mounts drew closer.

He vainly tried to swallow.

A thought chilled him. He might be dead before sundown. If the ruthless Cable and his men had their way Monrow knew that he surely would be.

His vision cleared.

The mist was still all around him, though. Even the breeze seemed unable to destroy it. It had mocked him for days. Yet it had also mocked those who hunted him.

Then suddenly he heard the strange noise again.

A noise he was incapable of working out.

What was it?

Whatever it was, it was closer now than it had ever been. Monrow knew it was somewhere just beyond the curtain of swirling heat haze at the foot of the sandstone cliff face. He had never heard anything like it before. A weird sound like whispering sand as it passes across desert dunes. Yet he knew it was not the sand. This was something else. Something real. Something alien to his knowledge.

Mustering all his strength he forced his body up until he was on all fours. He spat in a vain bid to rid his mouth of the sand he had somehow managed to consume on his treacherous fall from the top of the giant dune behind him.

The sound lingered in his ears.

It chilled him to the bone.

He tried to ignore it but it was impossible.

Monrow lowered his head and inhaled as deeply as he could and then tried to work out whether or not he had broken any bones during his crashing descent.

Each movement hurt but it did not appear to the stunned mind of the lawman that he had actually broken anything. He leaned slightly back until his bent legs were taking all of his weight, then he ran his fingers through his matted hair.

Monrow rested a hand on the sand and eased his left leg up until it was directly under him. Then he slowly rose to his full height and exhaled loudly.

He was still thirsty. So thirsty.

There seemed to be a thunderstorm inside his skull. It hurt more than any other part of his bruised body. He staggered forward, then stopped abruptly.

The noise became louder.

What was it?

Like a moth drawn to a naked flame Monrow began to limp towards the sound. Suddenly the border marshal remembered the shot which had caught his trailing leg at the top of the cliff. The wound where the bullet had passed right through his thigh was no longer bleeding. Like the rest of his lean body it had baked dry beneath the unrelenting sun.

Monrow continued onward. He resolved

that there was only one way to find out what was making those sounds and that was to investigate. He lowered his right arm until his hand found the holstered .45. His fingers curled around its grip. He drew it and checked its chamber. He replaced the spent shells with the last of the bullets from his gunbelt, then returned the weapon to its hand-tooled holster.

Again he thought of the approaching gunmen. He had six bullets and there were probably three times that number heading straight for him.

Monrow felt the breeze on his back as he started to move into the wall of moist haziness. His eyes began to see more clearly with each step. The swirling mist which earlier had dogged his attempts to see was much thinner down in the strange place he had found himself in.

He kept his index finger curled around the trigger of his gun in readiness. He knew that at any moment he might have to draw and fire.

A fevered mind had a way of creating

monsters where there were only shadows. He kept staggering forward. He had heard men called brave when in fact all they were was curious. Nothing was ever as it seemed to be. A million monsters might be waiting for him but he knew that most mythical creatures were only the figments of weary men's imaginations.

If whatever was making the eerie noise was dangerous he would have been dead by now. Whatever was creating the sound which drew him closer and closer had to be harmless, he reasoned.

A feeling of hope filled his chest.

He could hear the approaching horsemen now quite clearly, but he gave them little thought. He was on a voyage of discovery through the veil of mist.

Monrow moved faster, cleared the fog, then abruptly stopped in his tracks.

His eyes widened as they focused. 'Dear God,' he gasped.

17

There were answers now to questions the injured man had not even asked himself. Like a child's puzzle everything was falling into place. The hideous sight filled the border marshal's soul with a mixture of sadness and disgust. It ripped through him like a straight razor. Monrow staggered another few steps and then inhaled deeply. The breeze had kept the stench of death from his flared nostrils until this very moment. Now it hit him hard and he recoiled as though he had been shot.

For a few endless moments the young man did nothing. Not even think. He had seen a lot more death in his life than he cared to recall but there was something tragic before him which reminded him of the war. He knew how a lot of brave men were often regarded as heroes. They thought nothing of blasting towns with heavy artillery, never seeing the innocents who tasted their deadly venom. Few of those brave men ever saw the consequences of their actions.

Monrow had.

He had seen the pitiful bodies not only of men but of women and children as well. Witnessed what those balls of destruction did to living things. The severed limbs scattered as plentiful as leaves from trees in the fall.

Now the border marshal was staring with wide-open eyes at something which seemed no less horrific. Even the fading light could not conceal the truth from his gaze. The sandy slope was stained with the blood of those who had been cut down by the bullets of Cable's riflemen far above.

This was death where there should not be death.

Defying his own revulsion he limped forward. A thousand flies had already beaten him to this place but he did not notice them. All he could do was look down at the scene before him and wonder.

As always Monrow had to find out for himself.

A moccasin on a small foot was poking out from under the crumpled body of a heavily decorated pony. It was the only clue that this animal had not died alone. The adornments were unlike any he had ever seen before. They had to be native, but again they did not resemble any he knew of.

The pony lay on its side. The sickly aroma of rotting flesh filled his nostrils. Decay was swift in El Diablo. Monrow's attention was drawn to the haunting sound. At last he had the answer to the question which had been burning into his craw for what felt like an eternity. He now knew what had been making the strange noise which had chilled him to the bone for so long.

He paused above the broken legs of the Indian pony and looked down upon the unusual wooden rigging that was still secured to the harness of the animal just above its shoulders. It looked like a harp but Monrow knew of no Indians who adorned their horses with such things. It had two pointed sides resembling the horns of a steer. A fine rawhide twine was set between the horns. On the twine countless ornaments hung so close that the slightest movement caused them to touch one another. As the gentle canyon breeze swept over them they gave out a haunting melody.

It was musical and yet chilling. It was the music of the dead and Monrow had never heard its like before.

He removed his gloves, pushed them between his belt and pants and then rested his knuckles on his hips. Monrow glanced up before returning his gaze to the piteous pony. He could see bullet holes in the side of the dead creature. At least five stray shots had hit this animal.

Rifle bullets.

Monrow knew that this once well-ornamented pony had been hit by the ferocious bullets of Cable and his followers as they had blindly fired their Winchesters high above the place where he was now standing.

The dead animal showed all the signs of a creature that had fallen from a great height. Its bones protruded from its torn flesh. Its legs had shattered and were splayed. It was a sickening sight to a man who had lost his own precious horse in this unforgiving land. Monrow cast his eyes over what lay before him again.

Then to his utter surprise he spotted the one thing he had thought he would never see again. A large water bag made from the bladder of a buffalo or some other large animal lay a few feet from his boots. It was swollen with the precious liquid he craved. He rushed to it like a man possessed and plucked the bag off the sand. It was still cold. Still somehow intact.

Monrow removed its carved bone stopper, took a long drink and then carefully replaced the peg back into the neck of the bag. He lowered it back down on to the sand and felt the water making its way down into his parched guts.

Nothing had ever felt so good.

His entire soul was being dragged from the brink of death by the simple consumption of the liquid. Every part of him began to respond to the life-giving water.

El Diablo would have to wait a tad longer for him to die, he thought silently. There was a couple of gallons of living in that bag. He would savour every last drop of it.

Again he forced his eyes downward. Forced them to look hard at the other dead thing before him.

His heart ached.

She had been an Indian. That was obvious. Maybe twenty years of age or less. It was hard to tell how attractive she might have been before death had claimed her. Her face was dry. Cheeks sunken in.

Then the reverberating sound of the

riders approaching down the canyon drew his attention. Monrow turned and stared into the mist. They were coming after him, just as they had been doing for the previous three days. Cable would never quit, the marshal thought. Never quit until he knew for certain that he and his followers had done for another lawman. Monrow's fingers surrounded the grip of his handgun, ready to draw it.

Then suddenly another sound filled his ears.

Monrow's unblinking eyes burned down at the death before him and focused hard. A young woman had been crushed by the pony as it had fallen down into the deep crevasse, yet the sound had not come from either of these fly-covered bodies.

The young lawman stretched his injured leg until it cleared the neck of the horse. His boot rested only a few inches from her face. Monrow had to block out all the other noises and concentrate.

Then he saw it.

A crude box-shaped bag still on the young woman's back. Its rawhide tethers were still holding its precious burden firmly against her lifeless spine.

The sound was weak but Monrow had recognized it instantly.

He dropped to his knees and clawed at the crudely sewn bag until he freed it from her lifeless body. There was urgency in his fumbling fingers now as he tried to free the baby who could be heard whimpering weakly. Monrow pulled carefully at the brightly coloured blanket inside the basket and held it to his chest. Gently, his hands pulled back the blanket to reveal the small baby. He was no expert in such matters but reckoned the baby to be newborn. Only days old at most.

'Damn it all,' Monrow sighed and smiled at the face. 'How in tarnation ain't ya dead, little 'un?'

He rose to his feet, staggered to where the water bag lay, and eased himself down beside it. Carefully Monrow eased the child free of the blanket and quickly checked it. To his relief there seemed to be no broken bones.

Monrow dragged the large water bag up between his outstretched legs and removed its stopper. He dipped his fingers into the cool liquid, then placed them on the lips of the baby. The baby soon managed to suck the moisture from his wet fingertips.

'Tastes good, don't it?' Monrow whispered. 'Better than a barrel of sour-mash sipping whiskey.'

The breeze stiffened as the sun disappeared over the sandstone wall behind him. An eerie bluish light filled the chasm. The strange wind chimes on the harness on the dead horse grew louder.

Monrow kept on dipping the fingers into the neck of the water bag and placing them on the infant's mouth. He knew that Cable and his cronies would be upon them soon and would, more than likely, kill the both of them.

The sound of the unearthly chimes

seemed to be getting louder as the light faded around him. Now only the stars and the moon cast any illumination into the chasm. A black shadow, spread away from the sandstone wall against which they rested, would be their only protection from the riflemen when they eventually arrived.

'Reckon pretty soon we're both gonna get ourselves a one-way ticket to meet up with our mommas, little 'un,' Monrow said as he thought about the six bullets he had in his six-shooter. 'But I'll try and protect you as best I can.'

The haunting chimes grew even louder — so loud that they drew Monrow's eyes from the baby to glance upon them. For a moment he just stared at them, then he realized that the chimes were not getting louder at all. Not the ones he was staring at, anyway.

The hairs on the nape of his sunburned neck began to tingle. They were warning him that all was not as it appeared to be.

Monrow remained seated with the water bag between his legs and turned his head to look in the opposite direction. He could hear Cable and his men heading towards them.

The mist was thinner now but still dense enough to hamper even the sharpest of eyes from penetrating its ghostly movement.

Monrow screwed up his eyes.

A frightening realization dawned on Monrow. There were more chiming noises coming from beyond the fog. The baby's mother had not been alone in this desert. She had kinfolk and they had come looking for her and the child.

Then he saw strange shapes appearing through the mist.

He felt his heart quicken. He placed the palm of his right hand over the baby's head.

'Who is it?' Monrow croaked. 'Who are ya?'

Then the horses and riders cleared the swirling mist. There were at least twenty of them and probably more beyond his line of sight. Each horseman had the exact same rigging standing high above the shoulders of his highly decorated mount. The sound of their horses' rigging was far louder than that made by the one on the dead pony near him. Then the riders came to a halt and fell silent.

Whatever tribe they were, he had never seen images of them before. He had seen plenty of pictures of Apaches but these silent men were not Apaches. They appeared to be of some unknown tribe of wanderers.

Monrow continued to hold the child close to his sweat-soaked shirt. He could feel the baby's small heart beating against his chest.

Suddenly it dawned on the star-packer that the horsemen might not understand that he had had nothing to do with the death of the young woman.

Terror swept through Monrow. What if they assumed that he had done this to the dead woman? What then?

Three of the horses moved closer to

where Monrow sat with the baby in his arms. They were watching him as they also observed the dead woman.

Monrow noticed that none of them had rifles or sidearms but they did have small bows. Bundles of arrows hung in leather satchels on either side of their mounts' shoulders. He had never seen so many arrows.

Monrow tried to rise, but it was impossible.

He was totally at their mercy.

The jeers of the approaching riders suddenly filled the chasm. Ford Cable and his seventeen rifle-men were now within minutes of reaching this very spot. The sound of thundering hoofs echoed off the sandstone walls.

One of the Indians dropped swiftly from his crude saddle and rushed toward Monrow, holding a circular shield on his left forearm. The lawman flinched and held the baby close in his protective arms.

The warrior was fully dressed. He looked briefly at the baby and then at the child's dead mother.

He said something in a tongue which did not resemble any language Monrow had ever heard before. The star-packer stared into the eyes of the man, who repeated his unfathomable words.

Monrow kept a protective hold on the defenceless baby as the man's hands tried to take the infant from the lawman.

'What ya saying?' Monrow vainly asked the brave.

The Indian turned and gave out an imploring cry. Within seconds another paint pony moved up to him. Monrow squinted through the half-light at the woman astride the sturdy pony. She looked older than the dead woman he had discovered only minutes earlier. Pain was etched into her starlit features. Monrow instantly sensed that this woman must be kin to the mother of the baby he held.

She held out her shaking arms and, without uttering a single word, urged Monrow to give her the baby. Then as the whooping voices of the approaching Cable and his henchmen grew louder she also made a strange vocal appeal.

Monrow understood.

She wanted nothing more than to take the baby to safety before the band of ruthless killers reached them. Monrow gave a nod and handed the baby to the warrior, who in turn gave it to the woman.

The woman cradled the child in the crook of her left arm as her right hand dragged the crude reins to one side. Her small feet kicked into the sides of her pony. The animal galloped back into the depths of the fog.

Wide-eyed, Monrow watched the Indian warrior leap on to the back of his own pony. The Indian stared at the lawman for the briefest of moments, then swung his mount around and followed the other pony.

Like living phantoms the rest of the riders expertly backed their mounts away from the spot where the marshal sat. They seemed to melt into the mist as though they too were made of nothing more substantial than vapour. By the time Monrow had managed to get to his feet they had disappeared.

Monrow steadied himself, then heard the sound of the rampaging riflemen screaming at the tops of their lungs. He swung on his heels and dragged his .45 from its holster.

Then the mist swirled and parted. Cable and his riders burst through it. They thundered past him and headed away in the same direction taken by the Indians only a moment earlier. Even in the eerie starlight Monrow could make out each of their faces as they rode past him. None of them had even seen the dead pony, let alone the very man they were hunting.

The echoing of their mounts' pounding hoofs lingered in the head of the injured lawman. He stared at the fog which seemed to return as soon as they had ridden through it.

Cable had sure fired them up, Monrow thought.

They were fired up for some killing.

Nothing less would satisfy them now. Monrow did not know any of their names but he had seen each of their faces in the main street of Panhandle when the shooting had started. Every one of those riders had tried to kill him then, and had been fired with the same determination through each waking moment since he and they had entered the desert.

It was their stray shots that had slain the pony and caused the death of its mistress. Monrow felt nothing but loathing for them.

He glanced at his six-shooter. There had been far too many of them for his remaining half-dozen bullets to handle.

He was willing to stand and shoot it out with anyone whom he considered little better than vermin, but how could a man do that when faced with so many heavily armed adversaries?

He cocked the hammer of the gun.

Monrow bit his lip and limped into the dust which still hung in the chasm where it had been kicked up by the hoofs of his enemies' horses.

It was insane, but the young lawman knew that he had to follow those riders and kill as many of them as he could before they managed to achieve their goal and kill him.

Monrow had barely taken a dozen faltering steps when suddenly the foggy wall before him erupted into deafening gunfire. The light of eighteen rifles blasting their deadly bullets flashed like lightning before the stunned border marshal. The dark sky seemed to be alive with shooting stars but these were no heavenly rods that he was seeing. These were coming from the ground and tapering into the sky from rifle barrels.

Screams, a mixture of rage and agony, filled the air as the barrage of shooting went on and on. The entire chasm was filled with the sound of conflict. Monrow had only just reached the very middle of the narrow sandstone fissure when another sound joined the others. It was the sound of fearful horses galloping away from the heart of the shooting. Before Monrow had time even to realize what was happening, a pair of snorting horses burst out of the cold mist before him. The eyes of the terrified horses were wide and unblinking as they crashed into the hapless lawman and sent him reeling.

Monrow fell on to his back and gasped as he watched the horses disappear from view. They had only been in sight for a matter of seconds, but that had been long enough for him to see the arrows embedded into their saddles and their flesh. It was also enough time to note that they had no riders astride them.

The raging battle continued. It was close, he thought. Maybe less than a hundred yards from the spot where he had been knocked to the ground.

The mist was now becoming icy but no less dense. He stared at the sandstone all around him as it started to sparkle with the frost he had experienced each night after sundown.

He forced himself back up.

Then, without warning, another four startled horses followed the others as they fled from the nerve-shattering gunfire. Monrow had to move like a bullfighter to avoid being knocked down and crushed beneath their hoofs. Again Monrow focused on the riderless horses. They were also riddled with arrows. He was showered in their warm blood.

There was a battle going on just ahead of him, Monrow reasoned. Yet he could not see anything except the flashes from rifle barrels through the impenetrable mist. It sounded no less daunting than all the battles he had somehow survived during the brutal war, yet he knew that this fight was different. This was a fight between bullets and arrows.

The ear-splitting noise was coming from only one side: Ford Cable's side. The Indians' projectiles made little noise apart from the humming all arrows make when sent through the air from a taut bowstring.

Yet even though it seemed to be a mismatched combat there were an awful lot of horses without riders passing him and that meant that the riflemen were not having it all their own way.

The lawman scrambled towards the roaring gunfire. He gripped his .45 and held it at hip level, just as another horse came hobbling out of the cloud of mist. This horse still had its master on its back, but there was no sign of life in the dead rider. The man was slumped with a score of arrows in his back. The horse was also carrying a few arrows in its flanks.

Monrow grabbed at the loose reins and forced the wounded animal to a standstill. His eyes searched the rider and his saddle for weaponry. The rifle was gone from the dead hands but a Colt was still holstered on a bullet-rich belt.

The desperate lawman hauled the body off the saddle and let it fall to the ground. Then he holstered his own gun and unbuckled the belt from the dead man's hips. He wrapped the additional belt around his slim waist, buckled it and checked the six-shooter.

Every one of the Colt's cylinders six chambers held a fresh unfired bullet. Another twenty or more spanned the length of the belt leather.

'Now it's time for me to settle the score with them damn sidewinders. And Cable,' Monrow said to himself and spat at the ground. With renewed resolve he ventured forward again. This time he had two guns. One for each hand. The knowledge that he had more bullets than he had enemies seemed to bring a new determination to the border marshal. 'Now I'm gonna give them Indians a helping hand.'

The further Monrow limped into the canyon the more the mist thinned out. Then it was gone, to be replaced by the acrid stench of choking rifle smoke, as what remained of Cable's men blasted their Winchesters at their unseen foes.

Monrow paused and watched the startled riflemen fire their carbines at invisible enemies hidden in the sand-coloured rocks that flanked them on both sides. With almost every beat of the lawman's heart he saw another of the men who had hunted him for three days plucked from his saddles by arrows.

Monrow squinted hard. The gunsmoke was no easier on the eyes than the mist had been. The light of the gibbous moon and the stars seemed to be having a mighty hard time even reaching the floor of the canyon as the repeating rifles volleyed their vain attempts to destroy the Indians, who had them well and truly pinned down.

The sandy floor was littered with arrow-speared corpses. Both men and horses lay in pathetic heaps as more and more arrows rained down from each side.

Then Monrow saw him.

Ford Cable was right in the middle of his few remaining riflemen. He was still seated astride his sturdy mount, firing blindly at shadows. Shadows where phantoms jeered their spectral mockery.

Somehow neither Cable nor his mount had been hit by any of the arrows which buzzed through the darkness like crazed hornets.

'Cable!' Monrow managed to scream out at the top of his lungs. 'Cable!'

The echo of the name seemed to vibrate all about them. Bo Fontaine swung his wounded horse around and levelled his long-barrelled weapon at the man with the gleaming star on his shirt. Then squeezed its trigger. A rod of exploding fire came from its barrel. The bullet cut through the desert air.

Monrow did not move.

He raised both his guns and pulled on their triggers.

As the rifle bullet tore a chunk of his flesh off his shoulder Monrow watched his own shots hit the horseman dead centre. Fontaine fell backwards over his cantle with his rifle still clutched in his lifeless hands.

The rider hit the ground hard.

Monrow staggered, then steadied

himself. The bullet had hit the shoulder of his gun hand. Pain ripped through his fingers.

Cable turned his own horse and looked to where the marshal was standing. A satisfied smile twisted across his evil face when he saw the blood pouring from Monrow's shoulder.

'Mr Monrow,' the burly horseman yelled out as two more of his men were skewered with arrows and went cartwheeling off their saddles to land on top of their white-haired companion. 'Have ya come to die? I'll oblige ya if'n ya want.'

Monrow gritted his teeth.

He was in agony but refused to allow Cable to see it. He gritted his teeth and clawed back the hammers on both guns. The last of Cable's men charged his horse at the injured star-packer but Monrow did not flinch.

He no longer had any fear of them.

Death was all around him again.

Monrow swung his right hand upwards and fired. He watched the rider's head explode into a scarlet mess of gore. Each droplet of blood sparkled in the cold air of the chasm. The thundering horse kept on running as its master fell from the saddle, hit the ground with one boot still in his stirrup. He was dragged like a rag doll along the abrading sandstone.

Now there were just two men in the long gun-smoke-filled chasm. Monrow and Cable were again facing one another, as they had done several times back in Panhandle. There was only one difference from those occasions: this time one or both of them was going to die.

For some reason the arrows stopped raining down from the bows of the Indians. It was as though they could sense that this was now no longer a fight but a long overdue duel.

'Just you and me now, Cable,' Monrow shouted. Blood poured over his wrist as his thumb pulled back on the hammer of his smoking Colt.

An ominous feeling swept over the horseman.

Suddenly Cable realized that he was

alone. Alone to face the man he had tried so hard to kill. The well-built man glanced around the steep shadowy sides of the chasm. There was no sign of the Indians who had expertly avenged the death of one of their own. It was as if there had never been any Indians at all, but the ground all around him told a different tale.

A hundred or more arrows littered the sand. Moonlight danced along their feathered flights and upon the blood-soaked ground. Most of the arrows were in the bodies of the men who had followed Cable into El Diablo. Some were in the injured and dead horses, whilst others just stood defiantly in the sand.

None had even touched Cable or his mount.

Cable inhaled deeply.

'Ya oughta be dead, Mr Monrow.'

Monrow nodded. 'I'll not argue with that.'

Cable felt the sweat pouring down his spine under his shirt and top coat. He tossed his empty rifle aside, then dismounted and stepped over the bodies of some of his dead men until he was no more than thirty feet from the bleeding lawman.

'How come ya ain't dead?' he yelled.

'I've always reckoned that there are two types of luck, Cable.' Monrow slid one of his guns into its holster and then took a step towards his foe. He stopped and frowned. 'Good luck and bad luck. I've always bin blessed with a darn lot more of the good sort.'

'Until now.' Cable could see that Monrow's right shirtsleeve was soaked in blood. Another smile found his face and showed itself. 'Ya running out of the good type of luck just like ya running out of blood, boy. That's ya gun hand that's redder than a whore-house lantern. Must be hurting mighty bad. Ya gonna have a mighty bad time moving that gun finger when the tendons start to seize up on ya.'

'Maybe.' Monrow sighed and slid his own gun into its holster. He rubbed his tin star with his left shirt-cuff and stared across the distance between them. 'Care to try ya hand at a spot of star shooting?'

'Shooting stars has always bin a weakness of mine, boy,' Cable admitted. He pushed his coat over his holster to reveal his gun grip. 'Don't mind if I do.'

Monrow glanced at all the death which surrounded them. He felt sick. Steam had started to rise from the dead and wind its way upward.

'Make ya play, fat man.'

A riled Cable went for his gun. Monrow did the same.

Both weapons cleared their holsters. Both thumbs clawed their hammers back. Both fingers squeezed their triggers.

Two plumes of gunsmoke encircled both men's weapons as lethal red-hot venom blasted from their gun barrels.

Cable buckled as the lawman's bullet found his heart and burst it apart. He toppled backwards. A cloud of dust rose from around him. At exactly the same moment Monrow felt another bullet hit his already torn shoulder. The violent impact spun him on his heels, then Monrow also fell on to the sand.

Monrow lay on his back staring up at the star-studded sky above. Then, through watery eyes he saw two shafts of light briefly cut across the heavens.

'Shooting stars,' Rafe Monrow whispered, and closed his eyes. He felt himself being dragged down into a place he had never visited before.

A place to which he had no desire to go.

A place where only the dead were welcome.

Finale

The last thing Monrow could recall seeing before he lost consciousness was the pair of shooting stars which had crossed the night sky high above him. After that he had been sucked down into a whirlpool from which he imagined he would never escape. There was no way of knowing how long he had spent in the grip of death but suddenly he found himself awakening.

Simply being alive came as a surprise.

The bright sun was rising off to his left. He knew it had still to be quite early because the sand still sparkled with the night frost. Yet this was not the desert upon which he had fallen wounded. This was a lush area that he recognized as being far above the parched desert.

He blinked hard and looked straight ahead. The trees were everywhere casting their generous shadows across the land spread out before him. How had he gotten to this place from the spot where he had fallen?

The question confused and troubled him.

He blinked hard and became aware that he was propped up on some sort of simple cot. Then he saw a shadow cross over his outstretched legs. For a moment he did not move a muscle, as if he were half-expecting to be bludgeoned or worse.

Yet there were no stunning blows dished out from an unknown adversary. Monrow relaxed and stared down at his legs and then to what he could see of his upper torso.

His wounded shoulder had been tended to. He looked at the crude bandages made of some sort of dried leaves that had been carefully wrapped around his shoulder and upper chest. Monrow managed to rise until he was seated on the edge of the cot.

Carefully he lowered his boots to the ground.

Where was he?

Monrow sighed, then noticed the water bag next to the cot. Enough water to last him more than a week. Then he noticed his arms and hands. They had been washed clean of the blood which had flowed like a waterfall from his hideous wounds.

Monrow was bewildered but eternally grateful. It was obvious that someone had saved him from almost certain death.

But who and why?

Then out of the corner of his eye he saw them.

The Indians who had taken the baby and then avenged its dead mother were standing less than twenty feet away from him, beneath the canopies of several trees.

He stared at them, wondering why they had brought him from the notorious El Diablo to this fertile land. This was a place where the sun did not torture those who were trapped beneath its unforgiving rays.

This was a safe haven. An Eden.

A warrior approached the seated

marshal. His face was expressionless as his eyes met those of the lawman. He gestured with his hands. Somehow Monrow understood every movement of the fingers and hands. He was being told that he had been brought from the desert to this place after they had tended to his wounds so that he might return to his own kind.

He was also being informed that they had known it was the riflemen's wild shooting which had brought about the death of the young baby's mother.

They had saved Monrow because he had tried to protect the newly born infant, even though it might have cost him his own life.

The Indian waved his hand at the rest of his watching people, and their number parted to reveal the young woman who had taken the baby to safety. She moved towards him cautiously, with the small blanket bundle in her arms. She crouched before him and showed him the infant.

Monrow could not conceal his relief

and happiness from any of the onlookers. He raised his left hand and touched the dark hair of the sleeping baby with his fingertips. He silently watched the young woman return into the bosom of the others. For the first time Monrow noticed the children amid the warriors and women. One by one they mounted their highly decorated ponies with their strange regalia of chimes across the animals' shoulders.

Monrow stood.

The Indians turned their mounts and rode over a small crest between the trees. As the last of them disappeared from view the wounded marshal noticed that they had left Ford Cable's horse tethered to a tree.

Still aching, Monrow picked the water bag up, carried it to the horse and carefully hung it from the saddle horn. Then, to his surprise, he noticed the blanket across the cantle of the saddle.

It was the baby's blanket.

He tugged the reins free, stepped into the nearer stirrup and slowly mounted the unscathed animal. Monrow gathered in the reins and stared at the dust left in the wake of the native horsemen. Whoever these people were they were headed back towards the deadly desert. A place where they would, he hoped, remain unknown and unhindered.

The morning sun glinted off the tin star pinned to his torn and tattered shirt. Monrow turned the horse and gently tapped his spurs. As Rafe Monrow headed north the now familiar sound of the Indian's haunting wind chimes washed over his shoulders and travelled with him.

It was a sound that he would never forget.

THE END

DERAILED

Owen G. Irons

An outlaw gang has kidnapped the Colorado and Eastern train, leaving the passengers afoot in a winter blizzard. Tango and Ned Chambers, the men hired to prevent such things from happening, are left alone on the frozen prairie with a wealthy widow and a brother of the US vice-president. Now all they have to do is recover the train, get through to Denver and bring to justice those responsible for the outrage, without allowing harm to come to their charges . . .

FUGITIVE RUN

Chet Cunningham

David West is a fugitive on the run, despite his innocence. He leaves Boston and heads for Junction Springs, Colorado. Here he meets detective Susan Kramer, who needs him to help discover the identity of her father's killer. When, eventually, the killer is nailed and brought to trial, West returns to Boston with his new expertise, determined to seek justice and catch the man who killed his fiancée. Can West avenge her death and once more find love?

SUNDOWN AT SINGING RIVER

Ty Kirwan

Gunfighter Jorje Katz rides into the town of Singing River to begin a new life. On arrival he discovers that the partner he had financed is long dead. With no money to his name, Jorje's only option is to become a hired gun in a war that is raging between two political factions in the town. Dragged back into his old ways, Jorje despairs — until he is appointed Sheriff. At last it seems that his dreams can finally be realised . . .

SILVER TRACK

Caleb Rand

Having travelled to a wild frontier town in search of answers about his brother's death, Ben Jody finds himself not only in the middle of a bitter conflict between rival railroad companies, but also accused by the Army of being a deserter. With his good name tarnished and the law hot on his heels, he has little choice but to run. On discovering who is responsible for his brother's death though, Ben decides to ride right into the face of danger . . .

NO PEACE FOR A REBEL

Peter Wilson

The Civil War over, retired soldier Ethan Cole joins a group led by his former major, Daniel Reno, unaware that he's being drawn into a plot that could change the course of history. Believing he owes Reno his life, he goes along with the major's plan to stage a gold bullion robbery. But later, when Cole learns that Reno has a sinister goal in mind, he tries to prevent a war — and a vicious showdown with a former friend.

A MESSAGE FOR MCCLEOD

Emmett Stone

Tom McCleod, pursued by three riders, learns that a young woman he once knew has disappeared. Where is Sandy Kruger? Riding with Cherokee George, McCleod sets out to find her. She's escaped from the Cinch Buckle ranch, but is being relentlessly hunted down. Can Sandy survive in the wilderness? As he follows a dangerous trail, McCleod will need his wits and his guns if he is to find Sandy in time.

1	2	3	4	5	6	7	8	9	10
11	12	13	14	15	16	17	18	19	20
21	22	23	24	25	26	27	28	29	30
31	32	33	34	35	36	37	38	39	40
41	42	43	44	45	46	47	48	49	50
51	52	53	54	55	56	57	58	59	60
61	62	63	64	65	66	67	68	69	70
71	72	73	74	75	76	77	78	79	80
81	82	83	84	85	86	87	88	89	90
91	92	93	94	95	96	97	98	99	100
101	102	103	104	105	106	107	108	109	110
111	112	113	114	115	116	117	118	119	120
121	122	123	124	125	126	127	128	129	130
131	132	133	134	135	136	137	138	139	140
141	142	143	144	145	146	147	148	149	150
151	152	153	154	155	156	157	158	159	160
161	162	163	164	165	166	167	168	169	170
171	172	173	174	175	176	177	178	179	180
181	182	183	184	185	186	187	188	189	190
191	192	193	194	195	196	197	198	199	200
201	202	203	204	205	206	207	208	209	210
211	212	213	214	215	216	217	218	219	220
221	222	223	224	225	226	227	228	229	230
231	232	233	234	235	236	237	238	239	240
241	242	243	244	245	246	247	248	249	250
251	252	253	254	255	256	257	258	259	260
261	262	263	264	265	266	267	268	269	270
271	272	273	274	275	276	277	278	279	280
281	282	283	284	285	286	287	288	289	290
291	292	293	294	295	296	297	298	299	300
301	302	303	304	305	306	307	308	309	310
311	312	313	314	315	316	317	318	319	320
321		323	324	325	326	327	328	329	330
		33	334	335	336	337	338	339	340
		3	344	345	346	347	348	349	350
			354	355	356	357	358	359	360
			364	365	366	367	368	369	370
			374	375	376	377	378	379	380
			384	385	386	387	388	389	390
			4	395	396	397	398	399	400